# *Christmas in Little Penhaven*

# Christmas in Little Penhaven

Angela Britnell

*Where heroes are like chocolate – irresistible!*

Published 2021 by Choc Lit Limited
Penrose House, Crawley Drive, Camberley, Surrey GU15 2AB, UK
www.choc-lit.com

A CIP catalogue record for this book is available
from the British Library

ISBN 978-1-78189-453-8

Printed and bound in Great Britain by Clays Ltd, Elcograf S.p.A.

*I'm so happy to dedicate this story to Kendall, my wonderful new daughter-in-law in celebration of her first Christmas as a member of the Britnell family!*

# Acknowledgements

Thank you to the supposedly fictional inhabitants of Little Penhaven, led by the stalwart Cynthia Bullen (if you haven't read *One Summer in Little Penhaven* then rush to correct that soon and get the full measure of her) who insisted they weren't done having their story told and felt that everyone needed to see how they celebrate Christmas! And of course special appreciation to the amazing Tasting Panel members who agreed with them and knew Jane and Hal's story was special: Bee M, Sharon D, Gillian C, Michelle R, Wendy S, Carol D, Alma H and Sharon W.

# Chapter One

*Hark the Herald Angels Sing*? Jane sighed as the piped music drifted through the shop. There were still six interminable weeks left until twenty-fifth of December which, by her reckoning, meant she had at least another two hundred and forty hours of forced listening to Christmas carols. And that was only at work. Jane's mind wandered while she restocked the baked beans. Crushed by Christmas. Haunted by a Herald. Attacked by an Avenging Angel. Those might work as possible titles in her distinctly un-cosy mystery series. The series that so far consisted of one unpublished book. Minor detail.

After staying up writing until the early hours of the morning every day for the last month, she had squeezed in under the deadline by a matter of hours and entered a national competition for debut mystery writers. Simply thinking about the top prize made her heart race – representation by a well-known agent and a publishing contract. In her fantasy world she'd win and everything about her life would change, but reality was a different kettle of fish. Her obligations wouldn't disappear at the wave of a publisher's magic wand.

Her mobile phone buzzed and she did a quick check around her before pulling it out of her pocket. Marlene Hughes was the duty manager today, and the sour-faced woman wouldn't hesitate to report Jane if she caught her taking a private call during work. She couldn't afford to lose her job because year-round ones were few and far between in Cornwall, especially for someone who'd left school at sixteen with only a couple of lame GCSEs.

Remember SAPs tonight. 7pm. No excuses x

She had missed the last two meetings of the Little Penhaven "Single and Proud" (SAP) club but if she didn't turn up to this one her friends would track her down and drag her to the Queen's Head pub for a good-natured gossip and the pub's "Two for One Tuesday" deal where they'd drink their weight in wine.

I'll be there x

Although it meant a mile-long trudge each way in the dark it would be worth the effort to have a bit of fun for a couple of hours. She'd been friends with the original five SAPs for nearly twenty years, since arriving at the secondary school in nearby St. Petroc as a painfully shy fifteen year old who knew nobody. Heather, Kate and the twins Lisa and Pat had grown up together in Little Penhaven which meant they stuck together at school, and because Jane's new home was on the outskirts of the village they quasi-adopted her.

'All right, Jane?'

Philip Bunt leaned over her shoulder and flashed a friendly smile. 'Would you like a ride home when we get off at five? You'll get soaked walking to and from the bus in this lousy weather.'

He knew she rarely drove her car to work to save money. They'd started work at Freshlands together five years ago and become good friends. At regular intervals he asked her out, never appearing perturbed when she equally routinely turned him down. Now he was an assistant manager and she'd been guilty once or twice of considering whether "nice enough" was enough.

Jane tossed an imaginary coin in the air. 'Okay.' That sounded mean and grudging. 'Thanks.'

'I'm parked in the normal spot. See you later.' He loped off, whistling tunelessly.

She crossed her fingers he wouldn't read too much into her acceptance, but turning into a drowned rat wasn't her favourite way to end a dreary work day.

'Fine, give me Sam's phone number.' Hal Muir caved in to his parents' pressure. Now he'd be forced to repeat the idiotic story he'd concocted after bailing out of his successful gym business in California. He doubted his cousin would say it wasn't convenient because the Muir family tended to stick together. 'I don't know why you're fretting so much. I told you I sold my share of the business for a decent amount of money and my financial advisor is on top of things.'

'That's not what I meant son, and you know it.' His father's husky voice cracked. 'You keep tryin' to brush off that … trouble with Kristen Weeks. What happened to her wasn't your fault—'

'—I don't wanna talk about her, okay?'

'Can't you at least wait to leave until after Thanksgiving?' His mother intervened. 'Would it be so terrible to stay a couple more weeks? Everyone's goin' to Mary Ann and Preston's as usual and they'd all love to see you again. It's been far too long.'

As if he needed reminding. 'I prefer it this way, okay? Plus I reckon a complete change of scenery will help with the book.' Hal ignored the swift wordless glances his parents exchanged.

He punched in the long international number. 'Hi, Sam?' She couldn't have been more surprised when he explained who was calling than if he'd claimed to be the President ringing from the White House.

'Wow, it's great to hear from you. I haven't seen you in forever. How's it goin'?'

He sucked in a deep breath. 'Pretty good. I've given up the gym business to try to write a novel and need to get a kick start somewhere different.'

'Really?'

Clearly the idea of her jock cousin, no doubt more full of more swagger than brains in her memory, attempting such a thing struck her as ridiculous.

'Yeah. I've been doin' a bit of research on places to set my book and Cornwall looks pretty neat.' Hal had never even heard of the place until it came down the family grapevine that Sam married some guy from the far south west tip of England. 'Could I crash with y'all for a while?'

'I guess so, but you know we're expecting a baby in January? How long were you thinkin' of staying?'

'I'm not sure maybe a couple of weeks. Just until I find my feet.'

'Sounds as if you're followin' in my footsteps.' Sam chuckled. 'Just don't end up in Scotland.'

His cousin's story was now etched into Muir family lore. She'd been a corporate lawyer on assignment in London and was screwed over on an expected partnership offer. After a chance encounter at a London train station she ended up in Cornwall where she met a local farmer, Cadan Day, and the rest was history.

'Come whenever you like. We've plenty of room.'

4

Hal's throat tightened. Sam barely knew him from Adam. They'd been teenagers when they last met, and his athletic skills hadn't impressed her the way they did everyone else. The fact she could throw a football almost as good as he could and run rings around him academically too hadn't been a balm to his over-inflated ego. 'Cheers. I appreciate it. I'll let you know when I've booked a flight.' He ended the call and plastered on a fake smile for his parents' sake. 'She's good with me coming.'

Now to pretend an interest in becoming the next James Patterson while he worked out what to really do with the rest of his life.

'Sorry I'm late.' Jane apologised, yanking off her wet mac and shaking out her hair.

'We were about to give up on you.' Heather grabbed her arm. 'How's your mum?'

'Not too good today. She overdid it trying to clean the bathroom so her knee is swollen and sore.' On top of fixing their tea when she got home after work Jane also had to dragoon her teenage brother into doing his homework – his reluctance was becoming an everyday occurrence. She struggled to get her head around that, because she would have given anything for his opportunities.

'Come on, we've got the drinks in.' Heather took her arm and steered her towards their usual table at the back of the pub.

The other day they'd been joking that soon their group name would be redundant. Kate and Timothy got married last year, Heather would be next up the aisle in the spring when she married Terrence "Mole" Burrows, and Pat was now dating a fellow teacher. That left Pat's twin sister Lisa and Jane as the lone holdouts.

She squeezed in between Lisa and Heather on the long wood bench and straight away knocked back a large swig of wine. 'Sorry, girls I needed that.'

'No apologies needed. Now y'all listen up I've got news.' Sam beamed and cradled her pregnant belly with both hands. They'd inducted the lively American as an honorary SAP when she and Heather became friends, and now she rarely missed any of their get-togethers.

'Don't tell us you've cracked and found out if you're having a boy or a girl,' Kate joked, because everyone knew Sam's husband was adamant about keeping it a surprise. No one poked too deeply into his reasons but guessed they were tied up with the loss of a premature baby boy with his first wife, a subject everyone steered clear of for Sam's sake.

'Don't be ridiculous, that's not happening. There's a cute man comin' to Little Penhaven soon for Jane and Lisa to fight over,' she announced with an air of triumph. 'My cousin Hal is payin' me a visit, I'm taking a guess he'll probably arrive sometime next week and—' Sam winked at Jane '—you might have the edge on nabbin' him because he's writing a book.'

A deep flush heated her skin.

'It's weird saying this about family but he's pretty darn hot.' Sam held out her phone.

The huge man with his gleaming white teeth, thick dark blonde hair, bright blue eyes and muscular arms folded over a massive chest positively oozed cockiness.

'He was running a string of successful gyms where he

whipped all the Hollywood celebrities into shape. When we were teenagers he was a bit of a jerk but ... don't judge a book by its cover, right?' Sam's eyes sparkled. 'How's yours coming along anyway, Jane?'

It was on the tip of her tongue to tell them about the contest, but she wanted to enjoy the secret satisfaction of finishing her first novel a while longer. 'I'm still working on it. It's a long process.' A tiny omission but not an outright lie – so why did she feel so guilty?

Probably because guilt was her default emotion. These days most of it centred on the snatched hours she spent hunched over her laptop writing instead of helping her mother around the house or chivvying Nick along with his schoolwork. She was sixteen when her mother needed help in raising her new-born half-brother after Ralph Davy abandoned them, and since then she'd slipped into the habit of putting herself last. But even after her dreams of becoming an English teacher had to be shelved, Jane's love for words and literature never faded. A couple of years ago, when faced with a rude customer at Freshlands, she'd spent the rest of her shift mentally contriving ways for the annoying woman to meet her demise. She'd scribbled down her ideas later and they slowly evolved into the plot of *Crushed in Cornwall*, the first book in a planned series starring Henrietta Morley, her quirky Cornish detective. Writing had become her escape from everyday life and no matter what happened she couldn't give it up now.

# Chapter Two

Hal frowned at the narrow stream of water trickling out of the shower. If he wanted to wash anything from the chest upwards he'd have to bend at the knees and crouch. He and Cadan were pretty much the same height so God knew how the Cornishman managed.

From what he'd seen when Sam drove him through Little Penhaven yesterday, the small village wasn't much bigger than his fancy estate in Malibu with its own cinema, pool, golf course and collection of guest cottages. *You mean the fancy estate you used to own.* Gene Brock, his partner in the "Pumping Gold" gym franchise, was bewildered when Hal asked him to buy out his share of the business. They'd started with one building in a questionable area of Los Angeles and built it up over the last fifteen years into a multi-million dollar investment.

'Why?' Gene had asked '*We're raking it in and, despite that business with Kristen Weeks, anyone with any name value in Hollywood still comes to us. Put it behind you and move on.*'

He'd given up trying to explain that it wasn't that simple. The actress's death had no long-term effect on their profit margins so in Gene's opinion it didn't need to be rehashed and brooded over: the two things Hal had done day and night for the last year. Every time he walked back into the gym he pictured the paramedics dragging him off of Kristen's lifeless body. He'd been unable to accept that CPR wasn't going to get her breathing again. The fact that a police investigation cleared him of any wrongdoing was irrelevant. A woman died under his care. End of story. If he'd stayed at "Pumping Gold" he would have lost his mind. When Hal had tossed in the estate as an added inducement, his old friend hadn't been able to resist. Despite having enough money to live off for the rest of his life Hal didn't plan to be idle but needed to find a new focus.

Wandering back into the bedroom, he dried his hair and gazed out of the window. Hal felt like Dorothy in *The Wizard of Oz* when she realised she wasn't in Kansas any more. Cornwall couldn't be more different than Southern California. A patchwork of rolling fields stretched out into the distance with some cleared ready for spring planting while others were filled with grazing cows or sheep. Narrow roads wound through the countryside and linked the occasional houses and farms. It all looked a bit bleak and the village hadn't struck him as the last word in excitement either. Through yesterday's heavy rain he'd spotted a motley collection of shops, a church, a pub and rows of solid granite houses. It might look more appealing in better weather, but he wouldn't place any bets on that. His cousin Sam on the other hand preached the virtues of Cornwall to anyone who would listen. 'The coastline's real pretty here and there are amazing walking paths all the way around,' she'd said. 'Some are right on the cliff edges and scary, but the views are awesome. You'll love seein' the cute little ole fishing villages too. We've nothin' like it back home.'

Hal needed to hurry up and get dressed because the plan was to eat lunch at the Queen's Head pub in the village, run by Cadan's younger brother and his wife. He tugged on jeans and a long-sleeved T-shirt, then added a thick blue jumper to stop from shivering. Thank goodness he'd thrown in a few winter clothes, something he only needed in California when he went up into the mountains. The bloody walls in this old place must be a foot thick and, if there was any central heating system, it had no doubt been installed back in the Dark Ages.

Last night it had taken three attempts to find his bedroom after dinner because the rambling old house resembled a maze with different parts added on throughout the million years or so it'd been in Cadan's family. Okay, maybe that was an exaggeration but Cadan had boasted yesterday that he was the tenth generation to live at Gweal Day. He'd bet anything it had never sported anything like the gaudy outdoor Christmas decorations that made him smile when he arrived – the ones his cousin must be responsible for. Sam's parents always put theirs up on Thanksgiving but she'd beaten them to it by a few days, possibly to make Hal feel more at home. The irony didn't escape him.

Hal glanced down over the first landing.

'Ready for the off?' Cadan beckoned him down. 'Jory's saving us a table but Saturday's their busiest day.'

'You'd better give me a quick rundown. Who're all these people I'm gonna meet?' In the gym he always kept on top of "his homework". Keeping tabs on his clients was a huge part of knocking them into shape, because if someone was struggling with their gruelling workout schedule it paid to know they'd lost out a big movie role or been taken to the cleaners in a big-money divorce. He carried this through to his everyday life as well.

'Loaded question,' Cadan quipped. 'Half the village could be there and we know them all.'

'If you're up for walking down we can talk on the way?' His cousin came to join them. 'I want to hear about your crazy writing plans.'

'Leave the poor bloke alone. He doesn't need you interrogating him when he's too jet-lagged to think straight.'

*Thanks pal*, thought Hal, grimly.

'Come on, mate.' Cadan grabbed his arm. 'Let's get a good pint of beer down you. The world won't seem so bad then.'

Simplistic, but he'd give it a try.

Sometimes she was too soft for her own good. Being grateful for Philip's lift home the other day didn't mean she should have agreed to this lunch invitation.

'Jane, my 'andsome get us a pot of mincemeat when you're in the village.' Her mother limped out from the bedroom. 'I fancy a few mince pies.'

'But it's only the middle of November!'

'So what? I could eat them year round especially with a good dollop of cream.' A faint smile eased the strain in her prematurely lined face. The blame for that lay firmly on Ralph Davy's shoulders. Her mother had been struggling to bring Jane up on her own since losing her husband in a car crash and had been vulnerable to the charms of the handsome, smooth-talking, much younger man. Ralph hadn't wanted a teenage step-daughter and the feeling had been mutual. When her mother fell pregnant, it should have been a relief when Ralph panicked and packed his bags, but he'd "accidentally" pushed her mother down the stairs on his way out of the house and left her lying unconscious on the floor. By the time Jane returned from school and called for help, the damage was done. The doctors managed to save the baby but could do little for her mother's right knee.

'I know you could.' Jane laughed. 'If you can wait until Monday, I'll bring some home from Freshlands.' The stacks of Christmas cakes, puddings and all the other so-called essentials were already in place to help their customers survive the festive season. 'Do you want me to make you a sandwich and a cup of tea before I go out?'

'No, I'll do it myself. You go and have a good time. Philip Bunt's a nice boy.' A satisfied smile brightened her mother's face. 'I bet he's got a few pounds in the bank.'

'I couldn't care less if he has.'

'Then you should.' Val snorted. 'Only people with money say it doesn't matter.'

'I need to get ready.'

'Don't forget that even decent men are all after the same thing, and once they get it you don't see them for dust.'

Would it reassure her mother to discover that Jane was probably the most buttoned-up thirty-five year old in Cornwall? If you discounted a quick fumbling attempt at sex with her first real boyfriend, Andy Barker, so long ago she could barely even remember what he looked like, she was too afraid of the potential consequences to allow any man to get too close either physically or emotionally. Lonely but safe. An accurate description of her life.

'Don't worry, Mum.' The sudden knock on the door startled her. Trust Philip to be early. Oh well, he'd have to take her in old brown cord trousers and a baggy green jumper now. If nothing else, her lack of effort should confirm that this wasn't a date but simply two friends eating lunch together. She fixed on a smile before opening the door.

'Hello,' he greeted her. 'I hope it's okay if we go to the Queen's Head? I know it's your local but I've heard the food is pretty good there these days and I haven't had a chance to try it out.'

She bit her lip and struggled to hide her dismay. The locals loved to gossip and one sighting of her with Philip and people would have the banns read and St. Piran's church booked for the wedding. 'Of course, it's fine. Fliss is an amazing cook.' Jane admired the young woman and wished she had half of her gumption. Everyone knew Fliss wasn't simply born with a silver teaspoon in her mouth but a whole dinner service. She had left all that behind when she fell in love with Jory Day.

On the short drive into the village they chatted away easily, and she didn't object when he took hold of her hand as they crossed the street into the pub. The feeling of someone looking out for her for a change wasn't unpleasant.

Plainly Hal was the curiosity of the week. Make that the year. He'd been the subject of pointed stares and equally pointed questions ever since they stepped into the old pub.

'Welcome to the Queen's Head. I'm Jory Day. This one's *much* younger brother.' The grinning young man slapped Cadan's arm. With his shaggy blond hair, colourful shorts and sandals he more closely resembled a Californian surfer rather than the clichéd pot-bellied, ruddy-faced landlord of Hal's imagination. 'Hey, Fliss love. Come here.'

An elegant blonde woman, dressed in chef's whites and holding a laughing little toddler on one hip joined them and, despite her super-polite, friendly greeting, Hal knew he was being assessed again as Jory made the introductions. 'This little chap's Kit.'

'Yoo-hoo, Jane.' Sam suddenly waved across at a young woman who walked into the pub. 'Jane is one of the group of girlfriends I hang out with. We're called the SAPs, as in Single and Proud which everyone was at some point. A couple of us are married now and two more are on the downward path. Jane's still fancy free though and real cute. Hal, you'll love her.'

*Seriously?* He'd been here less than twenty-four hours and his cousin was matchmaking already? Sam's expression altered and he spotted the cause of her annoyance. This particular Jane came with a Tarzan attached. A tall, lanky man had his arm draped around her shoulders, but the dark-haired young woman appeared to step away to shake him off.

'Jane, this is my cousin Hal.'

'Oh, right. Pleased to meet you.'

The tall man was introduced as Philip Bunt, and Hal noticed his narrow face tighten when Jane blithely dismissed him as a friend and work colleague. And Jane Solomon? A million miles from the tanned, leggy blondes he dated in California but something about her stirred him. When she scrutinised him with her dusky blue eyes and a bloom of heat flushed her pale, freckled skin he couldn't look away.

'Earth to Hal.' Sam waved a hand in front of his face. 'You and Jane should get together sometime and swap notes on the books you're writing.'

'Books?' Philip frowned.

'Our Jane is all set to be the next Agatha Christie.'

'Don't be ridiculous I scribble a bit that's all.' Her colour deepened.

'Yeah, me too.' What the hell had made Hal say that?

'But you've put your job on hold to write. That's brave,' Jane said.

'Ask me again in a few months and we'll see.' The lie tightened its hold on him. Jane didn't immediately respond, and he suspected she saw right through him.

'It was nice to meet you. We're going to get our lunch now, but I'm sure we'll see you around.'

As soon as they left, Sam pounced.

'What do you think of Jane?'

He clamped down on the questions he wanted to ask. The last thing his cousin needed was any encouragement.

# Chapter Three

'Hi Jane, I need advice on which mince pies to buy.'

Hal Muir's distracting drawl took her by surprise, and she bumped her head on the shelf trying to stand up. Crazily, all she could think was why she was never dressed even remotely smart when they met? There was no hiding her garish bright green and yellow Freshlands overall while he, of course, looked drop dead gorgeous. Again. His dark jeans were stretched over legs that could surely bench press ... she'd actually no clue of an appropriate figure because her idea of working out was walking as much as possible to save money. Hal's black leather jacket had that buttery soft touchability gained over time and the white shirt peeking out at the collar drew attention to his rich, golden skin. The only people usually flaunting tans like that in late November here were the wealthy who could afford winter holidays in the sunshine, world class surfers or sun bed addicts.

'Mince pies?'

*Get a grip and answer the man*, she thought to herself.

'Apparently Sam used to be obsessed by some special English candy bar, but they turn her stomach now and instead she'd got a craving for these things.' He held out two boxes. 'The village shop is all out until the end of the week, so I offered to come on a mission of mercy before she tore our heads off.'

'Poor Sam. She did love her Crunchies.' Jane grinned. 'I'm not the best person to ask about mince pies because I'm weird and hate them.'

'Isn't that un-British or something?' An adorable dimple creased his chin.

'Probably.' She pointed to the box in his right hand. 'Those are my mum's favourites and she's a mince pie fanatic. Often she makes her own, but I doubt Sam will expect you to go that far.'

'I sure hope not. Cooking isn't my thing.'

'What is? Apart from writing. Sam mentioned you used to run a gym.' Always too observant for her own good, at least according to her mother, she picked up on a slight hesitation before he smiled again.

'What time is your lunch break? Is there any chance you might take pity on a stranger to these parts and join me for a bite to eat?'

She briefly wondered why he'd avoided answering her question before responding. 'It's in about ten minutes, but I only get half an hour.' Jane spotted Philip heading their way. 'I'll meet you outside and we can go to the sandwich bar next door. Go and buy your mince pies.'

'Yes ma'am.' He flicked a salute. 'I'm supposed to get somethin' called clotted cream too. Where—'

'Aisle two at the back next to the milk.' She almost shooed him away and briefly leaned against the shelf with her eyes shut.

'Aren't you feeling well?'

Philip's concern irritated her. If he wasn't careful, he'd be the next victim in *A Cornish Casualty*, the new book she'd started writing last night. The bags under her eyes were testament to the fact she'd stayed up until one o'clock getting the first chapter down. When the words flowed easily she couldn't bear to stop. Work or no work. 'I'm fine.'

'Our lunch breaks coincide today. Do you fancy taking our sandwiches down to the park? It's nice and sunny and we'll be warm enough with our coats on.'

'Thanks, but I'm going to snatch a few minutes to write.' The lie trickled out.

'Of course. No problem. I can't wait to read your book one day.' Philip's enthusiastic support increased her guilt. 'I'll see you later.'

She returned to unpacking boxes of stuffing mix.

'So, is it only mince pies you've got a downer on when it comes to Christmas?' Hal was trying his best to steer the conversation away from his recently aborted career and his imaginary writing.

'You don't want to hear my annual rant about the over-commercialisation of Christmas. I'm not a fan of Christmas pudding, Christmas cake or sherry either – the other staples of the British festive season.'

Her broad smile kicked him in the gut. Jane Solomon didn't need any artifice to outshine all of the groomed-to-the-last-fake-eyelash women he'd been surrounded by for so long.

'Even the SAPs shut me up if I get started on it these days.'

'Y'all are good friends. Sam told me about the group, I know it means a lot to her.'

'Me too. They are the best and I'm lucky to have them.' A shadow crossed her smile. 'I suppose Sam told you about my family?'

He hurried to reassure her that heart-to-heart chats with his cousin hadn't been on the agenda. Sam was far too busy finishing up the last house she and Cadan would renovate before her baby arrived. 'She's frustrated because she's torn between longing to have her baby and growing their new business. Poor old Cadan's driving her crazy because he's worried about her overdoing it. He found her up on a ladder yesterday painting a ceiling and really laid into her. They were all right later though. I kinda get where he's comin' from after Sam had a quiet word with me about his ex-wife.'

'I'm sure once the baby arrives safely, they'll be okay.' Jane toyed with her sandwich. 'Tell me about your book. I don't often have the opportunity to meet other writers and it can be a lonely process. You must know that, I'm sure. But when it's going well there's nothing quite like the satisfaction is there?'

As a small boy he'd discovered that winning people over with his easy smile and "aw-shucks" blond-haired, blue-eyed charm was a cinch, but Jane's quiet question rendered him helpless. 'I wouldn't know. There is no book.' He exhaled a heavy sigh. 'I'm pretty certain there never will be.'

'No book? But Sam—'

'—I lied. To her and my folks.'

'I don't get it.' Jane frowned. 'Writing a book is bloody hard work. Why would anyone say they're doing it if they aren't?'

'Because I'd chucked in the gym business … for various reasons I'd prefer not to go into today, and it sounded dumb to admit I'd no idea what to do next.'

'And that was the first thing that popped into your head?'

'Yeah.'

'You're out of your mind.'

'Probably.' Hal twitched a smile. 'I was calling my folks from the Los Angeles airport to let them know I was flying back to Knoxville and spotted a bookstore.' He shrugged. 'It just popped out. You won't spill my secret, will you?'

'No. But Sam is bound to suss you out. Nothing gets past her.'

'Yeah I know. She's a smart cookie but if I can just get a bit of breathing space, that will do. Then I'll tell them all the truth. I appreciate you playin' along.'

'There you are Jane, I've been looking for you.' Philip Bunt appeared out of nowhere.

'I'm not late, am I?'

'No, but someone rang the shop to talk to you because you weren't answering your mobile so I said I'd try to find you and you weren't in the break room.'

'Who called?'

'Jenny Pascoe. Your mum was in her shop and didn't feel well. I told Jenny we'd pick her up.'

'We?'

'I'll give you a lift.'

'That's all right. There's no need for you to leave work. I can run her over there,' Hal offered. 'Makes more sense. I'm heading back to Little Penhaven anyway.'

'Thanks.' She smiled at Philip. 'I appreciate you going to all this trouble.'

'Ring me later to let me know how she's doing.'

'I will do.'

Clearly Philip knew about whatever was up with Jane's

family, which shouldn't have made Hal feel resentful, but it did anyway for some reason.

Jane barely spoke while they made their way to the side street where he'd parked the pint-sized rental car, the only one they'd had available in Truro. After cracking a joke about folding himself into the vehicle and only getting a wan smile in response, he gave up and concentrated on navigating the narrow roads.

'Would you mind waiting outside while I fetch Mum?'

'Anything you want.'

She gave him a searching look. 'This sounds mad because I hardly know you, but I think you actually mean that.'

'I do.' Hal's assurance softened the strain in her face. 'Go on. I'll be here.'

'You know you can't walk this far, Mum.' Jane struggled to hide her annoyance.

'I know, love but I forget sometimes … or don't want to remember.' Val rubbed her swollen knee. 'I'd run out of mincemeat again.'

'Thanks for looking after her, Jenny.'

'That's all right my 'andsome. Me and your mum have had a good old natter, haven't we Val?'

Jenny had her faults, an overwhelming fondness for gossip being the main one, but she had a good heart. Sam could testify to that. The American would never have her fulfilling life in Little Penhaven if Jenny hadn't befriended her at Paddington station and convinced her to come to Cornwall.

'We've had a nice cup of tea together and mince pies with lashings of cream.'

*Oh well, that's all right then. Don't worry about me losing half a day's pay*, thought Jane.

'I'm sorry, love.' Val grabbed her hand. 'I'm a nuisance. I'm always messing up your life.'

'I never said—'

'You don't need to. I've relied on you too much all these years and it's got to stop. There's a lot you wanted to do with your life, and you gave it all up for me and Nick.' The two older women exchanged secretive smiles. 'Jenny's offered me a little job.'

'Job?' Jane tried not to sound incredulous. 'Doing what?' Shop work was hard. She should know.

'I know there's a lot I can't manage, but I'm not helpless.'

'I never said you were Mum, but—'

'—don't fret about it, my 'andsome,' Jenny interrupted. 'I don't have any problem being on my feet and Heather and her Terrence help with the heavy lifting these days. But we get proper busy sometimes and I could do with someone reliable to take care of the till and cover me when I want a break.'

'It will get me out of the house and bring in a bit of money,' her mother chimed back in.

One of them needed to be realistic. 'How will you get to and fro? The buses aren't very frequent these days and even if I'm available when you need a lift it costs a bomb to run the car.'

'I can chip in for petrol or someone else might give me a lift if they're on the way to St. Petroc.'

'I suppose you can give it a try.'

'You'm a good girl.' Jenny shoved a box of mince pies at her. 'Take those with you for later.' Her beady eyes landed on Jane. 'How did you get here anyway? Did Philip Bunt give you a ride?'

Lying wasn't an option because the observant woman would see them get into Hal's car. Her brief explanation made their eyes gleam, but she knew when they saw her hunky chauffeur their wild speculations would zoom off the charts.

'I'll come with you and say hello,' Jenny declared. 'Got to be friendly to our American visitors.'

With her arm hooked through her mother's, they made their way outside and when Hal leapt out to open the door for her mother flashing his killer smile as he did, Jane knew she was doomed.

# Chapter Four

If Hal explained that the home he grew up in wasn't much bigger than this small three-bedroom house, Jane probably wouldn't believe him. She'd been reluctant to invite him inside but her mother insisted.

'Jane probably wants to apologise for our Christmas decorations but I'm not going to.' Two red circles bloomed on Val Davy's cheeks. 'My girl would put them up on Christmas Eve and whip them down again on Boxing Day. I was going to wait at least another couple of weeks but I couldn't resist getting them out yesterday. They cheer things up I reckon'

The abundance of sparkling gold tinsel, Santa Claus ornaments of every shape and size and the overloaded tree topped with a fairy whose wand scraped the ceiling certainly came under that description. 'I gather she's not a mince pie lover either? You sure didn't bring her up right.'

'Please feel free to gang up on me, why don't you?' Jane's sparkling eyes reassured him that she'd taken his good-natured ribbing the right way. 'Have you ever even tried one?' she challenged. 'I'll stick the kettle on, and you can choke one down for your cheek.'

'Don't put the poor man off before he has a bite,' Val chided. 'Make sure you warm them up and give him plenty of cream.'

Hal suppressed the instant refusal springing to his lips. The words pie and cream didn't feature in the healthy eating regimen that had become an ingrained habit over the years. 'I promise I'll give an honest verdict.'

Jane scoffed and disappeared into the kitchen. The front door opened and a morose, lanky teenage boy sloped in, glared at Hal and tossed an overstuffed backpack on the floor. Val gave him a wary look.

'This is my son, Nick.'

'Who is he?' The boy glared at Hal.

'Hal Muir.' Hal held his hand out. The boy stared at it as though no one had ever offered to shake hands with him before. 'I'm Sam Day's cousin from—'

'You're a bloody Yank.'

'Not strictly speaking. Yanks are northerners. People from the south don't appreciate the label.'

'Mr Muir was kind enough to give us a lift up from the village,' Val explained.

'Why?'

Jane came back in carrying a loaded tray and Hal quickly offered to help her.

'Should've worked that one out, shouldn't I?' The boy scoffed. 'You're wasting your time mooning over my sister. She can't fit a boyfriend in between stacking shelves at that dumb supermarket and nagging us.'

'You're lucky she cares so much.' The pointed barb made Nick Davy's contrived surliness wobble. At seventeen Hal had that same dismissive attitude. He'd been a cocky, good-looking, high school football star who hadn't seen any further than the next game and the next girl.

'If you say so,' Nick muttered and dropped down on the sofa by his mother, succumbing with a grunt when she pushed the straggly curtain of jet-black hair out of his eyes.

'Tea everyone?' Jane offered.

'Yeah, sure.' Hal patted his stomach. 'Got to try one of these awful mince pies I keep hearin' about.'

'Ignore old misery guts. They're all right.' Nick crammed one in his mouth.

Hal bit into one of the small pies and the contrast between the spicy dried fruit mixture, sweet warm pastry and cold thick cream surprised him. He refused to think about the calories or fat content because it tasted so damn good. First thing Monday he'd start working out again. Easing up was one thing but becoming completely idle wasn't in his DNA. 'This is awesome.'

'Seriously?' Jane's bewilderment didn't totally revolve around his liking for mince pies. Hal had won her mother over straight away and subtly challenged her brother's stroppy attitude instead of tiptoeing around it. She was scared stiff that Hal Muir had woven his spell around her too. No doubt he was bored and needed something to enliven his visit to Cornwall, but she couldn't afford for that to be her. The fact Jane's family completely relied on her was simply how things were. 'You need your head tested.'

'You're not the first to say that. Problem is I'm not sure there's much in there to investigate.'

Under his easy good humour, she sensed a burning frustration and took a guess most people didn't see past his male-model good looks to the undoubtedly intelligent man underneath.

'We'll see.'

'Will we?'

Jane plonked her barely touched tea mug on the tray.

'I'd better clear up. Nick's got homework to do. He can't afford to let up this year. His future depends on it. I'll see you out.'

'But poor Hal hasn't finished,' her mother protested.

'It's okay, Mrs Davy. I'm good. I don't want to hinder y'all.' He jumped up. 'Good luck with the studies, Nick.'

The sound her brother made could have meant anything, but Hal simply nodded. She followed him to the door.

'One minute. Give me that much.'

Acutely aware of the heat emanating from him as they stood too close for her comfort, Jane longed for him to touch her while silently begging him not to.

'You sure are messin' with my head.' A frown knotted his brow.

'You barely know me.'

'Yeah, that's the whole problem.' A tiny glimmer of a smile returned to his puzzled gaze. 'How about us goin' on a date Saturday night?'

'A date?'

'Yeah, you know those things single people go on when they … are interested in each other.' He stroked his hand down her cheek, sending a shiver coursing through her body. 'Am I right to assume you are too?'

'Interested?'

'Yep. And single?' She caught a tempting hint of spice on his warm breath. Tempting on him. Not so much in a mince pie. 'Put me straight if you and Philip Bunt are—'

'—friends. We're good friends. That's it.' Jane's firm response elicited a broad grin.

'Does he know that?'

'I've told him enough times.'

'Not sure he believes it, but I can live with that … for now.'

The implication of something developing between them in time made her blush.

'Saturday?'

'I suppose we can.'

'I've received more enthusiastic responses from women before.' Hal chuckled.

'I'm sure you have. On a run of the mill day you probably have loads of them throwing themselves at you.' Her insecurity erupted and she wished for a smidgen of Sam's confidence. When her American friend set eyes on Cadan Day he hadn't stood a chance.

'Don't put yourself down. The world does that enough to us all. Don't join in.'

Jane almost asked what he knew about the subject but decided to save the question for another day. 'I'm working on Saturday until four and need to make tea for mum and Nick before I can go anywhere.' She might as well be upfront about her responsibilities now, so he didn't jump to any conclusions.

'How about I pick you up at seven?'

'That'll work. Thanks.'

'Thank you for givin' me a chance.'

*A chance for what?* she wondered. She was too afraid to ask.

# Chapter Five

'Stop smirking.' Cadan gasped for breath and clutched at his bent knees. 'We're not all fitness fanatics. I'm bloody knackered.'

'You were the one who said you were up for a run this morning.' Hal walked slowly along the garden path, stopping for the occasional stretch to keep his muscles from cramping.

'I didn't think you'd drag us all the way to St. Petroc. I'm surprised I wasn't reduced to crawling up Lanjeth Hill on the way back.'

'You nearly were, old man. If you'd gone any slower that snail I spotted would've passed you.'

'Real joker, aren't you?'

This was his effort to learn a reasonable balance when it came to physical activity. He'd always been an overachiever that way and it was one of the reasons for the success of Pumping Gold. His celebrity clients paid him well for not accepting their excuses but when Kristen Weeks died in front of him, he'd been forced to question that ethos.

Cadan flopped down on the bench and drained a bottle of water in one long swallow. 'I need to get back in shape to chase after this baby.' A dark shadow took the edge off his smile.

He sensed they were kindred spirits. Traditional men not given to expressing their feelings. He appreciated that his running buddy had asked very few questions since Hal arrived in Cornwall. Sam was a different kettle of fish. If she asked him one more time how his book was coming along, he'd end up telling her the truth to shut her up. That would open him up to a raft of advice because his cousin had inherited her mother's habits in that regard.

'I'm sure you've heard about Mikey and Andrea.' Cadan rubbed a hand over his smooth jaw. Yesterday Sam's pithy comment about whether he was growing a beard or simply lazy clearly had the required result. 'If I don't tell someone, I'll go around the bend.' A suspicious sheen brightened his clear blue eyes. 'It helps you're ...'

'Basically a stranger, plus I know how to keep my mouth shut? I could make a fortune telling the gossip magazines what I know about the celebrities I come into contact with, but personal trainers are like doctors and hairdressers when it comes to being discreet.' Hal noticed that Cadan didn't smile.

'I'm petrified of losing Sam and the baby.' Cadan's hoarse voice cracked. 'I'm spoiling this pregnancy for her ... for us both, really, with my irrational fears. It's driving a wedge between us and I can't work out how to put things right.'

'They're not irrational. Not with your history. Sam knows that and I'm guessin' it hurts her too, but she doesn't know how to help you.'

'You think so?'

'I'm no relationship expert so I might be talkin' through the back of my head.' *Understatement of the year*, he thought. At nearly thirty-seven the closest he'd got to committing to any woman was asking Lanie Drake to move in with him after they'd been dating on and off for a couple of years. A huge move in his eyes, but she'd burst into tears because he wasn't down on one knee proffering a sizeable diamond. 'I reckon you need to tell her what you've told me. Ask for her help.' He cracked a smile. 'They like that.'

'Maybe there's something to you …'

'Underneath the pretty boy looks?' Hal finished the sentence for him.

'Sorry, mate.'

'Hey, don't worry about it. I've used my appearance to further my own ends enough times.' His admission came with a shrug.

'You want to come and see what I'm working on in the shed? It's Sam's Christmas present.'

'Sure.' Hal sensed this was a rarely made offer. When Cadan and Sam married they started two businesses to maximise their joint talents. "Not a Holiday Home" was Sam's vision, although Cadan worked alongside her, and focused on renovating old Cornish houses. They let them out below market rate to local young people with an option for them to buy later. "Gweal Day Custom Furniture" was Cadan's real passion and, from the pieces he'd seen in the farmhouse, even Hal's untrained eye could see they were exceptional.

As they headed across the garden, he asked Cadan for ideas on where to take Jane on their date later that evening. Not knowing either the area or Jane's likes and dislikes made it a challenge.

'Jane? Does Sam know you've asked her out?'

Hal's face heated. 'I'm not sure. I haven't said anything but …'

'No doubt the SAPs have dissected it by now.' Cadan

gave his arm a friendly poke. 'You're a brave man. They're all protective of Jane because she's had rough deal in life.' His eyes narrowed. 'How much do you know?'

'Not much. We've barely had two minutes alone yet. I did meet her mom and brother. She's clearly got a lot on her plate.'

'Yes she had but I'm not saying any more.' He drew a finger across his throat. 'Just watch yourself and don't mess Jane around or the wrath of those women will come down on your pretty boy head.'

Hal took the good-humoured warning seriously.

'I asked Jory's advice when I didn't know where to take Sam on our first date and he nailed it.' He rattled off the details of the old pub in Mevagissey that had apparently wowed his cousin. 'The problem is all that old-world charm wouldn't be a novelty for Jane.'

'I want somewhere quiet so we can talk.'

'You can't go wrong with the Pier House in Charlestown. Ring them when we get back. We're still a month away from Christmas and there aren't many tourists around, so you should be able to book a table.'

'Cheers. I'm guessin' your evening worked out.'

'Certainly did. If her parents hadn't turned up unexpectedly at her house when we got back I would have ... um, been a happier man.' Cadan winked. 'That's all I'm saying.' He unlocked the shed and Hal followed him inside.

'Wow.' A small desk stood on a workbench and the dark polished wood lured him to run his fingers over the smooth surface. There was a row of tiny drawers, a sloped writing surface and compartments to store pens and letters.

'When Sam drags me around stately homes she always

lingers around the ornate morning rooms belonging to the ladies of the house. The fact she never sits still long enough to write a letter is irrelevant. I could've bought one but—'

'—the meaning wouldn't be the same.' A pang of envy clawed at Hal. He didn't resent Cadan and Sam's happiness for one second, but he suddenly realised that maybe he wanted it too.

Jane gritted her teeth and thanked Kate for the phone call. Now all the SAPs had done their duty. Ever since she bumped into Lisa in Freshlands and spilled the beans about her upcoming date with Hal she'd been inundated with "friendly advice". Just because she hadn't jumped into bed with a string of boyfriends didn't make her a complete fool.

She dragged out her two winter dresses from the wardrobe and took turns holding them in front of her. The choice was either the scooped neck plain black or the fine navy and green check. They were both years old, but she couldn't afford to waste money on something new with Christmas on the horizon.

'Sam's here,' her mother yelled up the stairs. 'Come and give her a hand. She's got some things for you.'

Jane threw the dresses on the bed and hurried down. 'What …?' Her voice trailed away at the sight of her friend standing in the middle of the living room with her arms full of colourful clothes.

'Nothing I've got would fit you, but we've trawled through everyone else's wardrobes to come up with these,' Sam declared. 'You'll need to carry this lot while I drag my whale like body up the stairs to sort you out.'

Laugh or cry? She couldn't decide. Jane should have been appreciative and grateful but hated that her friends knew she didn't have anything good enough to wear for a date with Sam's hot cousin. Her dismay must have shown because Sam's smile ebbed away.

'I don't learn, do I?' She nibbled her lip. 'I'm getting as bad as my mom. Blunderin' in and thinkin' I know best for people.'

'You mean well. All of you. But …' Tears stung her eyes.

'I'll take it all away again. Forget it.'

Poor Sam looked drained. Her swollen ankles and the dark circles under her eyes were clearly a testament to being kept awake at night by a lively kicking baby. But she'd dragged herself here because that's what good friends did. 'That's a pretty colour.' Jane pointed to a swatch of bright turquoise silk before another in a rich orangey gold shade caught her eye. 'So is that.'

'You don't have to be all British and "nice".'

'I'm not. I'm simply tempted.' *By these gorgeous clothes and your gorgeous cousin*, she thought to herself. 'Come on, let's see what we can find to fit me.'

'At least you're not reduced to wearing tents and stretched out leggings that could wrap around an elephant twice.'

In the bedroom Jane hesitated to strip off, not because she was bothered about the few extra pounds clinging to her waist and hips but from a reluctance to reveal her dowdy underwear. Sam wasn't an overly fussy dresser either, but Jane would bet anything she upped her game when she set out to seduce Cadan. Not that seducing Hal was part of tonight's plan, but it couldn't even be under consideration wearing a well-worn bra and knickers from the Truro market.

'These are my treat.' Sam dangled a bag from "Intrigue" in front of her face. The wildly expensive lingerie shop in Falmouth was way out of Jane's price range and she'd only ever dared to window shop there.

'I can't possibly—'

'—don't argue. Consider it an early Christmas present. Blame your mom if they aren't the right size.'

'My mum?' Jane's head swirled.

'Yeah.' Sam pallor disappeared under a blush. 'I kind of dropped you in it, I'm afraid. I tried to sneak a quick word with her in the shop, but Jenny overheard us and—'

'—oh God, you might as well have put an announcement in the *Western Morning News*!'

Tissue paper rustled and something black and lacy dangled near her nose. Jane snatched the low-cut bra and matching, almost non-existent, knickers from Sam's hand.

'I thought black lace was a safe choice.'

Safe? There was nothing "safe" about these gorgeous things. 'Isn't this a bit on the weird side? I mean Hal's your cousin.'

'Doesn't bother me and if he gets a peek at these, I'm pretty damn sure he won't care either. I think y'all would be good together. Get busy tryin' stuff on for heaven's sake. I'm meeting Cadan in the pub soon and he'll get his knickers in a twist if I'm late. Poor guy doesn't have a fingernail left for worryin' about me.' She rubbed her belly. 'The sooner this little one arrives the better.'

The moment she saw herself in the mirror Jane's

confidence did a nosedive. 'We haven't even kissed yet. This is … rushing things.'

'It'll make you feel good to know they're there. Doesn't mean you gotta do anythin' you're not ready for. And Hal's a decent guy.' Her eyes twinkled. 'He won't be here forever, though.'

Reality slammed into her. That was the main reason she didn't intend to seduce Hal Muir, or be seduced by him, tonight or any other night.

# Chapter Six

'I guess we're not gonna enjoy the romantic walk I'd planned around the harbour tonight?' Hal joked but Jane didn't respond, continuing to stare out through the windshield at the heavy rain beating down. They'd taken refuge in the car after leaving the restaurant.

In theory they'd had a good evening so far. His heart had jumped into his mouth when she opened the door to him earlier with her tempting curves poured into a deep amber silk dress. The gently plunging neckline and elbow-length sleeves were subtle but sexy enough to tie Hal up in knots. Cadan's recommendation of the Pier House proved to be spot-on because the food and service were both excellent. They'd discovered a mutual dislike of prawns and Jane introduced him to the delights of sticky toffee pudding. Apart from all that, the only direction they were going seemed to be downhill. They'd enjoyed none of the close conversation he'd hoped for, the swapping of life stories and getting to know each other.

'Probably not a good idea unless you want me to drown.' She tilted a smile his way. 'Which you might well do because I've been a complete bitch.'

'I wouldn't put it quite that …'

'… bluntly? Well you should. If one of my characters behaved this way, she'd be the next victim.' She exhaled a long, drawn out sigh. 'It's complicated. Sam put something into words this afternoon that I already knew deep down, but it freaked me out.' Jane gripped her hands together.

'She's responsible for all this.' She gestured down over herself. 'Her and the rest of the SAPs.'

Hal might not be the sharpest knife in the drawer, but he wasn't dumb either and couldn't make sense of a single word she was saying. Her colour deepened as she explained about borrowed dresses and new underwear. 'Wait … did you say black lace?'

'I'm not discussing that. Not now.'

It would be crass to admit that talking about that particular subject wasn't what he had in mind. Jane playfully smacked his hand and he seized the chance to sneak a kiss. Big mistake. The quick intake of breath he caught was his own but then she touched a finger to her mouth and gazed at him with her eyes wide with surprise. 'Is this what freaks you out?' he asked quietly.

'That's only a small part.' Her rueful smile was endearing. 'Not small exactly but in comparison to the other stuff it's easier to manage … Oh God I'm talking a load of rubbish.' Jane covered her face with her hands.

'Don't beat up on yourself,' Hal said. 'How about we start the evening over again?'

'I can't eat a second dinner or I'll burst out of Kate's dress. It took a lot of wriggling and swearing to get it on in the first place, but Sam insisted it would be worth it.'

'Full marks to my cousin.' His voice turned hoarse.

'I don't get it.'

'What?'

'You.' Jane sounded exasperated. 'It doesn't make sense.'

This time he simply waited.

'There's no way that any sort of "we" makes sense. Look at you and look at me.'

He did what she asked, with a touch of dramatic exaggeration thrown in. 'What's the problem?' Hal had a shrewd idea of the real issues bothering her but needed a way to make her see they weren't important. Or at least that they didn't have to be unless they choose to make them so. A sliver of exasperation crept in when she trotted out the "you're too good-looking to be interested in me" bit. 'For God's sake, listen to yourself!' Jane flinched but if she wanted honesty, she'd get it. 'To me you're beautiful but other people would still call you good-looking. They'd also call you intelligent, hard-working and loyal to your family and friends. What's more important?'

'You talk about me putting myself down, but you didn't build a successful business by being stupid and lazy.'

'Maybe not.'

'I don't know anything about your family and friends back in America. That's part of the problem.' She sighed. 'I'm rushing things … we're rushing things.' Jane tugged at her dress. 'This was a mistake. I'm not the holiday romance type.'

'Did it ever occur to you that I might not be either?' Hal grasped her hands and pulled her close enough that her subtle musky perfume surrounded him. 'I'll tell you anythin' you want to know. Some of it you won't like.' The warning made her mouth twitch with amusement. 'But you can have the whole darn lot if I get the same in return. Is that a deal?'

The narrow confines of the steamed up car, the monotonous soundtrack of rain beating on the roof and the heat pulsing from Hal's large body conspired to send

Jane's common sense zooming out into space. 'It's a deal.' She'd never seen anyone smile with what seemed to be every bone in their body before, but that's what it felt like when she saw Hal's face, and the effect was devastating. 'You could come back to mine for coffee if you like?'

'Yeah, that'd be great.' Hal rested his warm fingers on the curve of her cheek. 'We'll save the black lace. It'll be worth it.'

*I hope so.*

'And we'll come back to see Charlestown another day.'

'It's really pretty when it's not pitch black and tipping down with rain but it is winter time, so what do you expect?' Jane said.

'Crisp cold temperatures and a blanket of snow?'

'Very doubtful,' she scoffed. 'I could count on one hand the number of white Christmases we've had in my lifetime and most of those were nothing more than a dusting.' She gave him a sideways glance. 'You've a lot to learn about Cornwall.'

'I'm up for the challenge.' His bright blue eyes glittered. 'Home?'

'Home.' The eye-catching display of Christmas lights were blazing away cheerfully as they drove past Gweal Day, and she guessed Hal would be interrogated when he returned. Sam would pass Hal's verdict on their date around the SAPs and, later, her own phone would be buzzing. Conducting a romance in a glass house would be easier than trying to keep one under the Little Penhaven gossip radar. 'You can park outside our gate.' She frowned. 'Oh, that's the vicar's old Volvo. What's he doing here? I hope Mum's all right. Oh God, what if she—'

'—don't jump to conclusions.' Hal stopped the car. 'Let's go see.'

She opened her mouth to assure him she could cope, but his wary gaze shut her up. He expected her to push him away.

'Here, take this.' Hal draped his soft leather jacket around her shoulders. 'We don't want Kate's dress getting rained on.'

The moment Jane stepped through the front door she froze.

It wasn't hard to size up the situation because he'd been there himself. Replace his mother with Val Davy, white-faced and sobbing on the sofa. Put a sullen Hal in Nick's place after he'd been caught – insert the appropriate occasion here – drinking underage, smoking weed or tearing up his car in a drag race outside town on a Saturday night. The boy's greasy long hair hid his facial expression but his hunched shoulders and slumped appearance did the talking for him. A tall, thin, grey-haired man in a dark suit and dog collar was hovering over them.

'Oh thank goodness you're home, love.' Val clutched at Jane's hand.

'What's happened?' Hal asked.

The vicar glanced at him. 'Tim Farnham, I don't believe we've met.'

'Hal Muir, I'm Samantha's cousin and … a good friend of Jane's. Could you tell us what's goin' on?'

'I'm afraid I caught Nick and a couple of his friends vandalising the church and—'

'—don't be ridiculous.' Jane scoffed. 'I'm sorry, vicar but

41

you must be mistaken. My brother's been home all evening studying for his exams.'

Farnham pulled at the boy's sleeve to expose streaks of bright red paint. 'I'm truly sorry but they were spray painting swear words on the church door.'

'What's he talking about, Nick?' Jane pleaded. 'You were here and—'

'—oh, keep your bloody hair on. I went out, all right?'

'Surely you didn't do what the vicar's saying?'

'It's not a big deal.'

'Not a big deal?'

Jane's disbelief reminded Hal of his father. Jesse Muir could never get his head around the idea that any son of his would break the law and, worst of all, appear unconcerned about it.

'The other boys' fathers came to pick them up, but I know your mum doesn't drive and she said you were out for the evening so I offered to bring Nick home.'

'Thank you.'

'I'm afraid I'm duty-bound to report this to the church council and they may wish to take it further and report the damage to the police.'

'The police?' Jane's voice shook.

'Hopefully it won't come to that.' Farnham's face softened. 'We'll talk again in a day or two.'

Nick stared down at the floor until the vicar left.

'I want to hear everything. Now.' Jane's quiet anger filled the room.

When Nick stumbled to his feet Hal caught a whiff of stale cider on his breath. 'Can I have a word?' Hal steered Jane across to the window and lowered his voice. 'It's none of my business so feel free to tell me to butt out, but your brother's been drinking and—'

'—Drinking? Oh god, none of this makes sense.'

'I know, but it's late and your mom looks done in. I'd recommend you pack everyone off to bed and talk tomorrow. You won't get any sense out of Nick tonight and he'll be less defensive when he's sober.'

'I suppose you're right.' Jane turned back to her family. 'Let's all go to bed and we'll sort this out in the morning, okay?'

'All right, lovey. I'm sorry your evening got spoiled.' Val eased up off the sofa. 'Come on, Nick.'

For a second Hal expected the boy to protest, but he simply glowered as though that was expected of him and followed his mother out of the room.

'Sam will say this is typical of SAPs' first dates.' Jane's weak smile touched his heart. 'She and Cadan's evening ended abruptly when her parents turned up. Heather and Mole …' she tailed off '… let's leave it that. They made impulsive choices that night and questioned them in the morning.'

'Hang on to the fact that they all came through it.' He'd been aching to hug her all evening and gave in now.

'You really think we can too?'

'I reckon we've got a fighting chance. That's good enough for me if it is for you?'

'What exactly are you asking?'

'I'm not certain, but I reckon if we spend as much time as possible getting to know each other better we'll see what happens after that.'

Jane's tentative smile returned and a thread of hope sneaked into him.

# Chapter Seven

Why did Jane feel like a head teacher grilling two disobedient students? Her mother wouldn't meet her eyes and nibbled a slice of toast while Nick glowered at the kitchen floor. 'Right, who's going to start?'

'Nick said he was going to meet a couple of mates in the village and I couldn't see any harm in it.' Val sighed. 'The poor boy's always got his head stuck in a book or on the computer. I thought it'd do him good to get some fresh air. You're always harping on at him for not getting any exercise.'

'I hoped he might start jogging or playing football, not vandalising the church. I've done my best with him but I'm not his parent. You are. Do you think you might actually do the job for a change?' Her mother flinched. 'Oh Mum, I'm sorry I never—'

'—don't apologise. I'm the one who should do that.' Tears wobbled on the edge of her red-rimmed eyelids. 'I know a lot of things need to change around here. Most of them start with me.'

Jane managed to nod. If she tried to speak she'd end up crying. She turned to her brother. 'Your turn.'

'Gaz and Sprout asked me to meet them and—'

'—Gaz Menear and Sprout Hooper? Do you need your brains tested?'

'They're all right. They're my mates.'

She longed to shake her brother's bony shoulders. The other two boys were known troublemakers and had only escaped serious punishment because Gaz's father was a

44

prominent heart surgeon in Plymouth and Merlin Hooper a famous television actor. 'You know who they'll pin the blame on, don't you?' Nick turned pale. 'Whose bright idea was it to deface the church?'

'Gaz. He brought a few bottles of cider and we drank them in the churchyard.' A faint smile lightened his drawn expression. 'I didn't like it much and my head hurts like hell this morning so don't panic about sending me off to rehab. Sprout had a couple tins of spray paint so we thought we'd mess around a bit. Have a bit of a laugh.' Nick's brazenness faltered. 'I'm really sorry, Mum. I just wanted to fit in for once. Be normal.'

'What on earth do you—?'

'—shush, love let him speak.' Her mother's interruption silenced Jane and, for the next five minutes, she listened in silence as her dreams for Nick crumbled.

'For God's sake let me do that, Sam.' Hal snatched the string of lights away from his cousin. He'd caught her standing on tiptoe trying to drape them over the massive Christmas tree now dominating the living room. This morning Sam had declared that with only four weeks to go until Christmas there was no excuse to remain tree-less any longer. They'd visited a farm near Newquay where Sam spent an hour selecting the stunning Norway fir, before he and Cadan were tasked with cutting it down and tying it on the roof of the Land Rover. 'Cadan's bloody scared enough already without catching you doing this.'

'Scared? I know he's a bit on edge about the baby, but scared? What exactly are you gettin' at? Come on, spit it out.'

Sam's Southern accent broadened, reminding him so much of her mother he thought his Aunt Mary Ann had sneaked into the room while he wasn't looking. He mentally tossed a coin and came down on the side of family. Obviously Cadan hadn't followed through on his promise to talk to his wife about his fears. 'He's more than on edge, Sam. Can't you see it?' Hal had only known his cousin's husband a few weeks, but with each day that went by the poor man's expression became even more haunted. 'Why don't we sit down?'

'Because if I sit down I start thinking, and if I do too much of that I start worrying about Cadan as well as this little one.' Sam's voice hitched and she stroked her belly. 'I can't tell him I'm scared shitless of giving birth when he's wrestling with all these damn demons.' Her face crumpled and she started to cry. Hal pulled Sam into a tight hug, well as tight as possible under the circumstances, and held her until she fell quiet.

'Come on.' They sat on the sofa and he waited while she blew her nose and swiped at her red swollen eyes.

'I know all women are anxious about going into labour, but Cadan thinks I'm superwoman. My physical strength was one of the things that attracted him to me, and he loves that I've never met a challenge I didn't rise to. How could he ever understand—'

'—try me.' Cadan stood in the doorway with his arms folded over his chest, and Hal couldn't read his blank expression.

This was his signal to leave. 'I'll see y'all later. I'm off to see Jane.' He hadn't heard from her but would take a chance and turn up on the doorstep.

'Cheers, mate.'

'Oh yeah, cheers.' An edge of sarcasm tinged Sam's words. 'Go on with you.' Her slate-grey eyes softened. 'Jane needs someone on her side.'

He nodded and cracked a smile. Hal wanted to be that someone.

Jane didn't usually do clingy or weepy but succumbed to both now, clutching onto Hal's dark blue wool jumper and sobbing into the fuzzy warmth. 'All these years ... don't for a minute think that I resent it because I don't ... I happily put my life on hold so Nick would have the opportunities I never had.'

She repeated her brother's words to Hal. *You never asked what I wanted. School work's easy for me so it wasn't a big deal until I moved on to the sixth form when all I heard was that I'd better do well in my exams or I wouldn't get into a good uni and my life wouldn't be worth shit. All the time you're slogging away at Freshlands, coping with the house and Mum and everything. But you know what? I love Cornwall. I like living here. I don't want to be banished up country somewhere to fulfil your dreams.*

Hal listened as the story tumbled out and didn't immediately reply.

'You think I'm wrong too, don't you?

'Wrong? No. Not wrong.' He wiped the damp tears from her cheeks and planted a kiss on her mouth when he was through. 'One day Nick will realise the value of everything you tried to offer him but right now he's too young to appreciate it.'

She caught a hint of hesitation, unsure whether it was something he was afraid to say in case he offended her or a confession of his own that he might not be ready to share.

'My folks' world revolved around me. When I showed athletic promise, they nurtured it and poured time and money into giving me every chance to maximise my talent. Everyone assumed I'd be picked by a top college team to play football and then go on to the pros.'

'What happened?'

Hal grimaced. 'My cocky teenage stubbornness. I decided academic stuff was a waste of time and coasted in classes. I got bored of goin' to football practice every day and working out so started skipping it. It'd be easy to say I got in with a bad crowd but I'm tryin' to be honest here and the truth is I pretty much *led* the bad crowd.'

Jane struggled to hide her shock. It wasn't easy to rationalise Hal's tales about underage drinking, smoking, recreational drugs and sex with the apparently disciplined man he had become. The same one who had confessed to her that, until he ate mince pies at their house, he hadn't touched anything for at least fifteen years that wasn't part of a carefully designed diet. 'How did you turn your life around?'

'Threw a few things in a backpack and headed for California.' He quirked a smile. 'Sam must've learned her fleeing tactics from me.' Hal's good humour faded. 'I got it in my head that I needed to stay away from my family to keep myself on track. Maybe I did for a while but somehow the years slipped away. Oh, I kept in touch but only the bare minimum. Recently I was brought up short by certain things that ... happened. It made me realise—'

'—I might've guessed she'd bloody bring you here to lecture me.' Nick sloped in.

The sight of her brother scratching his unwashed hair gave her the violent urge to drag him upstairs and stick him under the shower. That irritated her almost as much as him interrupting when Hal was on the verge of opening up to her.

'I came to see your sister, but I'm happy to toss in a lecture if you want?'

'Don't bother 'cos I'm sure you agree with her. Education is the only thing blah, blah, blah. Expand your horizons. All the usual crap.'

'You got any plans tonight, Nick?' Hal asked.

'I'm probably grounded for the next ten years.'

'I was gonna take your sister out for a meal, but how about I take you instead? If that's okay with her of course?'

Jane read his questioning shrug as asking her permission to share his story with Nick. 'Do what you like. It could be the last time he goes anywhere for a while.'

Hal raked a scathing glance over her brother. 'You'd better clean up first. Most eatin' places prefer their customers not to resemble a health hazard.'

If she'd said the same thing, Nick would have given her a mouth full of cheek in return but he simply grunted and ambled off upstairs.

'Was that a "yes, sir I'll go shower and put on clean clothes"?' Hal quipped.

'It was the closest you'll get.' Jane popped a kiss on his cheek. 'Thank you.'

'It might not help.'

'It's worth trying a different approach.' She swallowed

back the tears tightening her throat. 'Everything I've done has failed.'

'It sure hasn't.' Hal gripped her shoulders. 'Underneath all that stroppy teenage angst, he's probably a good kid.'

Jane hoped he was right.

'When I bring him back later, you're comin' with me.'

'Where?'

A wicked grin spread over his face. 'Anywhere I can kiss you without interruptions.'

'I've heard Cadan's garden shed is a good spot.' Her face burned. 'I mean ... oh for heaven's sake, forget I said that.' Confidences the SAPs shared were supposed to remain secret.

'I'm an elephant. It runs in the Muir family. We forget nothing.' Hal winked. 'You can get some writing done while we're out.'

'If you're not careful a handsome, muscular American will meet a grisly death in the next chapter of *A Cornish Casualty*.'

'Ouch. You're a hard woman.' He glanced over her shoulder. 'You ready to escape?'

Nick hovered at the foot of the stairs and, for a moment, she saw him again at five years old dressed in his stiff new school uniform with his hair freshly cut for the first day of primary school. Now, at seventeen, he'd almost grown into his tall, lean frame and only a faint trace of acne scarred his pale skin. It struck her that Nick was on the verge of becoming a handsome young man and wasn't her baby brother any longer. She had never seen his striking resemblance to Ralph Davy so clearly before. Years ago she went along with her mother's wishes and they never mentioned him in front of Nick. Every time he asked about his father they gave evasive answers until his questions eventually petered out. But maybe they'd been wrong and were now paying the price?

'Where are you taking him?'

'Not sure but I think we'll avoid the village.' Hal's response made Nick colour up. 'Go on out to the car, I'll be there in a minute.'

Jane sensed a smart remark hovering on her brother's lips, but he shrugged and disappeared outside. 'Why doesn't he argue with you? If I ask whether he wants boiled or scrambled eggs he turns it into a full-scale battle.'

'I'm a step removed. There's no history or expectations with me. You gonna wish me luck?'

'Of course. Good luck.'

'I hoped for somethin' a little more … inspiring.' Hal jerked her closer. 'Yeah, that's better.'

'Do you always get what you want?'

He dragged a teasing kiss over her mouth before stepping away. 'I'll see you later.'

It was at least five minutes before Jane's heart rate slowed back to normal and she headed upstairs to take Hal's advice. She rarely had the house to herself but her mum was working in the shop for another couple of hours so she could settle down and get another chapter written. The other night she left Henrietta Morley stranded at the bottom of a deserted tin mine with a broken ankle, no signal on her mobile and a vicious storm brewing off the coast. Jane could rescue her but that would be too banal. Having the murderer track down the detective would be far more interesting to write and ratchet up the tension for her readers. *Her readers?* She couldn't actually imagine anyone ever reading a book with her name on the front cover. When her phone dinged, she idly checked for new emails and had to read the first message three times before daring to believe it. When she read the fine print, Jane groaned.

# Chapter Eight

'Dessert?' Hal offered Nick the menu. He'd forgotten how much and how fast teenage boys could eat. Being hauled home by the vicar and the fallout from his foray into vandalism hanging over him clearly hadn't affected his appetite. He'd waded through a thick charred steak and a mound of chunky French fries drenched in ketchup, refusing to touch the peas and grilled mushrooms that came with it. Nick had considered Hal's choice of grilled trout and salad seriously weird. 'You can go order for us. I'll have the—'

'—apple crumble and custard?' Nick scoffed. 'That's what I'm having. I'm guessing you'll join me, seeing as we're on some sort of bonding exercise?'

The sarcasm rolled off him. Hal had used the same tactic to deflect his parents' and coaches' attempts to make him see he was screwing up his life. 'Sure, why not?'

'You must really want into my sister's—'

'—stop right there.' Hal hissed. 'You're not gonna talk bad about Jane around me.' Nick's scowl darkened. 'Order our food and get me a coffee. Black.' The comeback he fully expected was restricted to a dismissive "whatever".

'It'll be about five minutes.' Nick returned and shoved a branch of an unwieldy Christmas tree out of the way to slide back into his seat, knocking one of the shiny red balls off in the process. 'Damn.' He scrabbled around on the floor to pick it up and stuck it back where it belonged. 'It's as bad here as our bloody house. Sit still long enough and you get decorated.'

They'd selected the Black Horse pub in Trewhale on the

basis of it being far enough away from Little Penhaven that they were unlikely to bump into anyone they knew, as well as because a decent number of TripAdvisor reviews recommended the food. So far they'd been proved correct on both counts.

'Your mom's into Christmas in a big way?'

'It's her thing.' The boy's tolerant grin reassured Hal that Nick's indifferent attitude only ran skin deep. 'Don't you Ya— I mean Americans go overboard for it too?'

Hal suppressed a smile at the swift correction but couldn't have come up with a better way to ease into his story if he'd designed it himself. 'It's hard to generalise because it's a big country but the Muirs are pretty big on the holidays. Sam's parents used to have a houseful of us over for Thanksgiving in late November. Everyone used to gather outside to watch her dad turn their Christmas lights on.' Hal chuckled. 'Wouldn't be surprised if you could see them from outer space.'

'You've missed it this year.'

'I've missed it for a lot longer than that. After I moved to California I couldn't afford to go back at first and then … I was tied up with my business.' If he couldn't be honest with Jane's brother, they wouldn't get anywhere. 'I made a lot of bad choices at your age and I'm still workin' on putting things right.'

'Two crumbles and one coffee.' The young waitress set down their order and treated Nick to a lingering smile before drifting off again.

'Friend of yours?'

'She goes to Truro College too. Her name's Demelza Carter. She's okay.'

'You should've spoken to her.' Hal winced. 'Sorry, mate. I was out of line there. You didn't ask for my advice on chatting up girls.'

'I could do with some.' Nick looked embarrassed.

The kid didn't have a father around. His mother seemed sweet but clueless. And Jane? Jane was too busy to cover the trickier side of navigating manhood. Sex-ed classes at school and "the talk" from his sister wouldn't have touched on a simple thing like making conversation. 'Happy to help. Start by simply being friendly. Ask about a class you take together or what she's reading out of school. She's just a person like you and most folks like talking about themselves. Don't come on too strong and frighten her off.' This was all advice he could have done with taking at seventeen. 'I was an idiot at your age. I didn't treat girls well and most of them took it from me because I was a good-looking jock where that was celebrated. I could get away with anything I damn well pleased.'

'You're nothing like I thought you were.' Nick shook his head.

'Is that good or bad?'

'Not sure yet. Anyway, aren't you supposed to confess your youthful screw-ups and set me right?'

*You asked for it, kid.*

Congratulations! You've been selected as one of six finalists in the Poisoned Chalice competition for your debut mystery novel, *Crushed in Cornwall*. The shortlist will appear in tomorrow's Guardian newspaper and the winner will be announced on New Year's Day!

Jane found herself reading the email again. Her fellow SAPs would be hurt to find out her exciting news that way and so would her family. Jane only saw two alternatives. The first was to buy up all the papers in Jenny Pascoe's shop without setting off the woman's gossip antennae, but that option was no doubt doomed to failure. The second choice involved her apologising and begging for forgiveness.

Half an hour later Jane sat on her bed and wept into her pillow. She didn't deserve such good friends. None of them condemned her for holding out on them and during an impromptu group FaceTime session Sam had declared Tuesday evening "Celebrate Jane Night".

'I've had a word with Fliss and she's setting the back room up for us. We're gonna have champagne, or nasty sweet sparkling apple stuff for those of us haulin' a baby around, and she's gonna fix your favourite lasagne,' Sam had explained, excitedly.

They'd expanded the guest list to include all of their men plus Jane's mum and Nick. A touch of awkwardness sneaked in when her brother's name was mentioned. The news must be all around the village by now and, despite loving Nick beyond anything, Jane couldn't defend his behaviour.

'We're back.'

Hal's deep voice boomed up the stairs and she raced down to wrap her hands around his neck, pulling him to her for a swift, hard kiss.

'Wow, I sure like the enthusiastic welcome.'

'I'm not sure I'm old enough to see this.' Nick smirked. 'I'm going to my room. I've got homework to do.'

'Really?' She couldn't believe her ears.

'I never said I was chucking it all in, did I?'

'Back to normal.' Jane shook her head when her brother stalked off upstairs.

'Not quite.' Hal gave her a quizzical look. 'Don't get me wrong, I love nothin' better than having a beautiful woman throw her arms around me, but I'm not convinced I earned it simply by being gone for a couple of hours. What's happened?' He touched her face. 'Your eyes are shining and if your cheeks get any redder we could use them for a Rudolph costume.' He trailed a finger over her lips. 'And your mouth has got delicious curves at the edges like you can barely stop smiling.'

'Read that.' She pulled out her mobile and showed him the competition message.

'Oh wow.' Hal's dazzling blue eyes glistened with pride and he plastered her with kisses.

'Sorry I didn't say anything before.' She tended to babble when overexcited but he listened to her rambling explanation with no sign of impatience. When she finished Jane invited him to the party, but he didn't answer right away. 'What's wrong? Am I pushing too fast? Is that some line I shouldn't have crossed?'

'It's not you—'

'—don't you dare to trot out that old line.'

'Now who's jumpin' to conclusions? I was only gonna ask if you reckon I'm ready for interrogation by the SAPs?' Hal's sardonic smile warmed her heart. 'I suspect they'll grill me like a well-done steak on the barbecue.'

'Just remember they'll mean well.'

'Southern women always "mean well" but they're worse than the CIA when it comes to winkling out information.'

There were questions she hadn't dared to ask yet. Anything to do with how long he was staying and what work he intended to do now he'd turned his back on his business in California was out of bounds. Then there was whatever he'd been about to confess the other night before Nick butted in. She'd never enjoyed being with any man this much and Jane would protect him from her friends' curiosity if necessary to give their growing relationship a fighting chance. 'Don't worry I'll warn them to back off.'

'You'd do that for me?'

'Do you need to ask?'

'Sorry.'

They still had a lot to learn about each other. 'Will you tell me what happened with Nick?' Her stomach churned when Hal's smile disappeared.

This would be a balancing act. She deserved his honesty, but he'd made a promise to Nick. One he couldn't break. 'Let's sit down.'

'Nothing good ever starts with those words.'

'It's not all bad. Trust me.' Always the act of touching her, inhaling her scent and sensing the imprint of her kisses on his mouth centred Hal. One day he'd find a way to tell her that no other woman had affected him this powerfully before.

'You told him your story?'

'Oh yeah, he knows me warts and all now.'

'I don't suppose you worked a miracle and changed his mind about university.'

'Not exactly but he agreed to a compromise if you're good with the idea.' Hal crossed his fingers. 'He'll knuckle down and work hard to pass his exams next summer then he gets a year hangin' around at home here but only if he's workin' somewhere and helping y'all out. But that means no—'

'—nagging. I have to back off.'

'I wasn't gonna be that … blunt. Is Sam's brashness rubbin' off on the SAPs?'

'Probably.' A trickle of humour softened her stern expression. 'I don't quite see how a year of doing what he wanted in the first place is supposed to make him want to jump on the first train out of Cornwall at the end of it and do something meaningful with his life though.'

'Hang on a minute,' he protested. 'That sounds like you're saying that your life doesn't have meaning?'

'I never said … this isn't about me.'

'Isn't it?' He suspected Nick had nailed a huge part of the problem when he complained that his sister was trying to live out her dreams through him. If he didn't tread carefully this could blow up in his face. 'Humour me for a minute and give me the potted biography of Jane Solomon.'

'I don't see what that's to do with Nick?'

*Exactly. But I want to help you too*, Hal thought. 'Please.' Hal listened quietly to her steady, unemotional recitation. Growing up with only a few vague memories of her father, it had turned her world upside down when her mother rushed into marriage with Ralph Davy and wrenched them from the only home she'd known in St. Agnes to live in Little Penhaven.

'I hated everything about life at that point.' A faint smile sneaked in. 'Until I met the girls at school. Heather, Kate,

Lisa and Pat saved me then … and they've done it over and over again since.'

'I'm sure it's a mutual thing. Y'all rally round for each other.'

'I feel I do a lot more taking than giving most of the time.'

'I'm sure that's not true. But why did you drop out of school early?'

'I wasn't planning to. I was all set to go on to the sixth form college and then to uni. I wanted to study English literature and teach.' Her face turned to stone. 'But I didn't have a choice after my mum got hurt and Nick was born prematurely. They needed me here.'

The rest of the story poured out and Hal's fists bunched up. What he wouldn't give for the chance to punch Ralph Davy. 'Why wasn't he charged?'

'Because Mum denied he pushed her down the stairs, so the police had nothing to go on.' Jane shrugged. 'She insisted it was an accident and maybe it was.'

'So you gave up your dreams, left school and went to work?'

'There wasn't any choice.'

There were always choices and a lesser person would have left her mother to raise Nick alone and continued with her own plans.

'I don't regret it. My family is everything to me.'

The hint of a challenge in her husky voice pulled Hal up short. 'I realise that. Mine are too but I've done a lousy job of showin' it and that's one thing I need to put right.'

'I'm happy to hear you say that.'

'We'll talk more about it another day. I promise. But right now, let's concentrate on Nick.'

'He is incredibly smart and the things he could achieve are limitless … if he doesn't limit himself. How do I sit back and let him throw that all away?'

'You've gotta trust him.' Hal rested his forehead against hers. 'Y'all are important to him too. He's young. Give him time to work it out.' He stroked her thick silky hair and caught the scent of lime and coconut from her shampoo. It stirred visions of a tropical island with Jane stretched out on hot white sand next to him in a tiny red bikini.

'Do I even want to know what you're thinking about now?' There was a tinge of colour on her cheeks. 'I suspect it's nothing to do with Nick.'

'Sorry.'

'You don't sound very sorry.' Jane's smile faded. 'I suppose I'll have to go along with all this, but it'll mean crossing my fingers for a bloody long time.'

'Isn't that what all parents do … or sisters in your case?' Hal realised that his folks must have held their breath for years until he survived his own rebellious stage. Soon he'd find the words to express his appreciation.

'I suppose so.'

'Now we've put the world according to Nick somewhat to rights,' Hal wrapped his arms around her, 'I reckon it's time to fulfil the promise I made earlier.'

'I … wish we could.'

'But?'

'Mum will be back home any minute now because Heather and Mole are giving her a lift on their way to Newquay.'

'And you don't want to risk leaving Nick alone here with her?' He saw that tears were glistening in her eyes. 'It's okay. You'd be surprised how patient I can be.'

'Maybe I'm the impatient one.'

'I can live with knowing that.'

'Keep me up to date with what you find out from the vicar and if there's anything you need from me, just ask.'

'Thank you.'

He trailed a lingering kiss on her mouth. 'We should make the most of these few minutes.'

'Now we're definitely on the same page.'

# Chapter Nine

Jane inwardly groaned as she watched the bags of shopping being unloaded on the kitchen table. Jenny Pascoe wasn't exactly losing out by employing Val because her mother had clearly turned right around and spent most of her first pay packet right there in the shop. Not on essentials either but on more boxes of mince pies, a fruit Stollen, mini Christmas cake bars and a chocolate orange.

'It's a dark chocolate one. Your favourite.'

Her mother shouldn't have to be defensive but they both knew how tight money was.

'I'm sorry. It felt good to have my own money to spend for once.'

'I know and I'm sorry for spoiling your pleasure.' They weren't great huggers but she squeezed her mum's shoulder. 'Let's put the kettle on. I can't resist trying the Stollen.' It didn't make sense that she disliked mince pies so much but loved the fruit-studded German Christmas treat. 'I've some good news to tell you. Look at this.' Jane's enthusiasm bubbled over as she explained about being shortlisted in the writing competition.

'I'm so proud of you. I don't know how you've found the time between work and all you do for us. You'm a good girl. The best.' Everything about her mother sagged. 'I don't deserve you. Not after I brought Ralph Davy into our lives and he ruined everything. It was like he knocked all the stuffing out of me when he …'

The breath caught in her throat. Would her mother

say the one thing she needed to hear? Not for revenge, because that time had long passed, but to loosen the grip his memory had on them.

'... knocked me down that day,' Val finished and shook her head. 'I know you'd like me to tell you for certain, but I honestly don't know if he meant to push me. We were arguing about him leaving and next thing I'm falling down the stairs. Afterwards I was so poorly, and it was touch and go whether I'd lose Nick, that all I could think about was that as long as Ralph left us alone and I had you, we'd be all right.'

'And we are.'

'How can you say that? Look at everything you've given up.'

For the second time Jane found herself defending her choices.

'You'm a good little liar.' Val struggled to smile. 'But I'm tired of being poor Mrs Davy that everyone feels sorry for. Better seventeen years late than never, right? Pour our tea and let's make a plan.'

'Yes, Mum.' A flicker of optimism surged through her and they were still laughing and deciding what they'd wear to the party when Nick poked his head around the door. 'Come on in. There's plenty of tea in the pot.' Jane couldn't blame him for looking wary. 'We've got a lot to talk about and it's not you.' He shrugged and flopped down next to her, flicking his hair out of his eyes. After he'd wolfed down a thick slice of cake and gulped half of his sweet milky tea she nodded to her mum. This wasn't Jane's story to tell.

'I've never talked to you much about your father. I

thought that was the best way years ago and Jane went along with me … but you're not a little boy any longer, and it's time you heard the full story.'

As Val's story emerged, Nick lost every scrap of colour.

'Where is he now?'

'I don't know my 'andsome but Jane's going to help me track him down.'

'They should lock him up for hurting you.'

'I've always told your sister I wasn't sure he meant to hurt me and I'm still not certain. I doubt I ever will be.'

'Doesn't matter. He still bloody left you there. You could've died. We both could.'

'I know but listen to me for a minute, love.'

All her mother wanted from Ralph Davy was a divorce and to properly move forward with her life. Jane had tried to warn her mum that Nick might not understand her decision to draw a line under that part of her life.

'Are you fuckin' serious?' Nick looked incredulous as Val explained her reasoning.

'Don't use that sort of—'

'—it's all right, Jane, he's got a right to be angry.'

'That's the first sensible thing you've said,' Nick yelled. 'The rest of it's a load of bullshit.' He shoved the chair back and jumped to his feet, slamming his hands on the table. 'You pair can talk as much as you like. I'll find Ralph bloody Davy and show him what's what.'

'You're in enough trouble already. Don't make things worse,' Jane pleaded.

'Worse? A stupid bit of vandalism at the church versus making my so-called father pay for what he did? I know which bothers me the most.' Nick's face was filled with anger. 'If I sit around and do nothing, I'm no better than him.'

'Sit down right now Nicholas, and listen to me for once.'

Her soft-spoken mother never raised her voice and always took the path of least resistance where Nick was concerned. He slumped back down in the chair while Jane stared at Val in shock. She'd aroused a parental dragon and it was breathing fire.

Hal was wandering along the corridor towards his bedroom when Sam flung open a door and poked her head out.

'We've finished the nursery. Come and see.' She beckoned him in. 'That's if we're not disturbing you writing the next great American novel?'

'Hardly.' Hal shoved a hand through his hair. Could he possibly be more stupid? 'Sam, I lied to my folks and y'all because I'm a damn idiot. I'm not writin' anything and I never was. I wanted to get out of California and the gym business for a whole lot of different reasons and made up the book thing as an excuse. You're smart. Didn't you guess? When I told Jane she was sure you would have done.'

'Jane knows?' He watched her smirk broaden. 'Silly question. I thought the idea of you writing a book was unlikely but we haven't been in touch in years so I thought you might've changed a whole lot. I expected you to get here and lock yourself in your room for hours tapping away on a computer or always be scribbling away in notebooks like Jane but when you weren't I've tried to give you the benefit of the doubt. You gonna tell me a bit more about why you made up such an idiotic tale in the first place?'

He was debating how much to admit when Cadan wandered out of the nursery to join them. Hal's embarrassment deepened when Sam immediately shared his confession. 'I'm really sorry.'

'It doesn't bother me.' Cadan shrugged. 'We've plenty of room and you're not exactly hard work to have around. You obviously needed to be here.'

'Maybe but I ought to clear off like I promised. You don't need me under your feet.'

'Go? Who said anythin' about goin'?' Sam's fierceness made him smile. 'If it wasn't for you, we'd still be acting as idiots and hiding our worries from each other.' She beamed at her husband. 'Instead it's all good. I'm not sayin' everything's perfect but at least we're not being dumbasses about it.'

Hal wasn't sure he deserved all the credit but his cousin didn't give him a chance to speak.

'Get in here and give us your opinion.'

'Mine?'

'Yeah.' Sam dragged him inside.

'Uh, looks great I guess.' A nursery was a nursery, wasn't it? A baby bed. Toys. Books. Clothes. Cute bunnies on the walls. Hal supposed it ticked all the boxes.

'I know you don't get it but that's okay.' Sam's face softened. 'Before we ... got on the same page about the baby we'd avoided sorting out the nursery.'

His throat tightened as she explained that Cadan and his first wife, Andrea, originally set up the room ready for their baby's arrival but after Mikey's tragic death and his parents' bitter divorce it'd been left untouched. It stayed frozen in time until Fliss and Jory moved in temporarily, when it was cleaned up ready for their son Kit to spend his first few months at Gweal Day.

'I hesitated to suggest any changes because I was afraid of hurting his feelings and he—'

'—was the same.' Cadan's weary smile hinted at what the memories still cost him. 'This is a compromise.' He gestured around the room. 'Like all the best marriages, right sweetheart?'

'Absolutely,' Sam agreed. 'We changed the blue walls to this pale yellow but kept the mural because Cadan painted it for Mikey and it's too cool to cover up.' The barely perceptible hesitation when she mentioned the little boy's name sent a brief shadow flickering across her husband's face. 'He's gonna do a new one on one of the other walls for our little one after he or she arrives. The cot and bedding are new, but Cadan made the bookcase and toy chest before and there's no reason not to keep them.'

'It all looks amazing and your kid's gonna be so lucky.'

'We're the lucky ones.' When Cadan tried to wrap his arms around Sam but couldn't quite reach they all laughed.

*You sure are.* Hal wasn't given to envying other people. He'd been largely content with the successful life he'd built for himself in California until an unsettling dissatisfaction crept in. His solitary existence had begun to grate along with a nagging unhappiness with the way he'd drifted away from his family. Kristen Weeks' tragic death had brought his growing disillusion with the Hollywood fitness business to a head. Since being in Cornwall he'd started to question far more than simply what job to consider next.

Meeting Jane was the catalyst and she had turned on its head his usual attitude towards women and relationships. Instead of enjoying a woman's company for a while and moving on when it suited them both to make a change, he found himself craving more. He'd dated enough beautiful women for Jane's looks to be relatively unimportant compared to her quick humour, agile brain, strong work ethic and dedication to her family.

'Are you still with us?' Sam poked his arm.

'Sorry I was miles away.'

'Back in Tennessee? I bet your mom's nagging you about goin' home for Christmas? The only reason mine aren't beggin' us to visit is because no airline's gonna let me fly. They're not too keen on delivering babies over the Atlantic Ocean.' She grimaced. 'Anyway, they've got their tickets booked to come over in mid-January for this little one's arrival.'

'Mom and Dad weren't expecting me anyway.'

His cousin's eyes narrowed. 'Yeah, you haven't been to any family gatherings in a while. What's up with that?'

'Work mostly.' *But not completely*, he thought. 'My clients needed me around to make sure they didn't slack off over the holidays. They couldn't afford to show up for filming on January first carrying extra weight.'

'Sounds grim.'

'Yeah, but even so I —'

'—don't you dare say it! I told you we're good with you staying.' Sam wagged her finger. 'If you don't hang around my poor husband will be stuck eating the massive turkey I've ordered pretty much on his own because this baby isn't leaving me much eating room now and in a few more weeks?' She rolled her eyes. 'I doubt I'll be able to squeeze in even one Brussels sprout.'

'You wouldn't anyway,' Cadan chimed in. 'Don't use the poor baby as an excuse. You hate sprouts.'

'Really?' Hal asked, surprised. 'They're an extremely nutrient-dense super food. Rich in antioxidants and a good source of—'

'—blah, blah, blah I don't care. They're vile. If you aren't careful, I'll change my mind and toss you out.'

'Message received and understood.' He flung up his hands in surrender. 'What about Jory and his family? Do pubs here open on Christmas Day?'

'Yeah, it's silly season for them. In another couple of weeks, it'll crank up and they'll be slammed from then until after New Year,' Sam said. 'Fliss's folks will be here for Christmas to see little Kit. They'll help with babysitting too because Kit's unofficial nanny, who happens to be their cousin, is going home for a few days. We would've helped out but—'

'—much as you hate to admit it, you can't keep up with Kit any more?'

His cousin stuck out her tongue.

'He's a lively little devil.' Cadan's pride shone through. 'He's a full-time job and I've got enough of those already with juggling the two businesses and trying to keep my lady from squatting down and having our baby in the middle of ripping out a bathroom.'

'I'm happy to help out with anything you need a hand with … bar cooking. I'm pretty hopeless around the kitchen.'

'I expect you lived on protein shakes and ready

cooked meals from expensive upscale health stores out in California.'

Sam's shrewd observation made him wince.

'Yeah, thought I'd nailed it.' She smiled knowingly but then suddenly grasped her stomach. 'Ouch.'

Cadan turned pale and Hal felt the blood draining from his own face.

'Oh, for heaven's sake, cool it!' Sam rolled her eyes. 'It's only another of the practise contractions everyone gets and perfectly normal. Get me a glass of water and I'll sit down for a bit.'

When her husband rushed off to the kitchen she turned to Hal.

'The poor guy's still a bit jittery and that won't disappear until the baby's here safely. It'll help us all if you don't freak out too.'

'Sorry,' Hal mumbled. 'This is new to me.'

'Yeah, believe it or not it is to me too.'

'You seem …'

'Calmer?' Sam picked up a white stuffed rabbit and idly retied the blue ribbon around its neck. 'Once we hashed things out my fears didn't disappear, but I treat them differently now.' Her eyes glazed. 'When I was fourteen, I badly wanted my dad to teach me how to tile a roof but then he finally agreed and I panicked. He talked me through the whole process. We covered all the safety precautions to take and what to do if things went wrong. I still had butterflies the first time but when I studied the new roof afterwards I was overwhelmed with pride.' Sam giggled. 'I reckon holding our new baby will top that.'

'It certainly will.' Cadan returned with a glass of water. 'It'll be awesome, and you'll be an incredible mum.'

'You can deny it all you want but I still say your kid's goin' to be damn lucky,' Hal declared. 'I'm off to bed. Don't do anythin' I wouldn't do.' He smacked his head. 'Oh yeah you already did. Too late.'

'We'll get our own back won't we, Mrs Day?' Cadan cuddled his wife.

'Oh yeah.' Sam's smile widened.

He scoffed, turned his back on their raunchy laughter and strode off.

# Chapter Ten

Jane hadn't had time yet to explain to Hal what happened after they parted company on Saturday night. It'd been remarkable to hear her mother stand up to Nick.

'I don't want to hear any of this "I'm the man of the house and it's my job to defend you" nonsense. You don't have to agree with my decision but it's mine to make not yours. Assuming Jane finds him for me I'll let him know how to contact you, but I wouldn't hold your breath,' Val had said firmly.

She'd sympathised with her brother's frustration but after he railed at their mother for a while he'd given in. A sign he was growing up? She hoped so.

'You okay?' Hal asked her.

'I'll be better when this is over.' They were wedged into the back of the vicarage living room because Tim wanted to hear first-hand accounts of the vandalism incident from all three boys.

'Cadan says Farnham's a good man. He reckons he'll push the church council to be lenient on them.'

'I hope he's right.'

'Hello, everyone.' Tim scuttled in, took off his glasses and rubbed them with a handkerchief before slipping them back on. 'I appreciate you all for making the time to be here on a Monday morning, but I really wanted us to have the chance to speak before the emergency PCC meeting tomorrow afternoon.' He fixed his gaze on the boys. 'The council rightly takes vandalism very seriously and even if

I ask them to be lenient, they may wish to go ahead and prosecute the boys. If they win the vote it will be out of my hands.'

'Look, Farnham, can we get on with this?' Merlin Hooper swept back his dyed blond hair, looking a lot older without make-up and air-brushing. 'I've got to catch the London train ready to start filming in the morning.'

'Yes, and I've got patients waiting to see me in Plymouth.' Dr Menear's booming voice filled the room. 'Merlin and I have discussed this. We're happy to make a generous donation to church funds and our boys will apologise. Goodness man, most of us have been reckless as teenagers. There isn't much for them to do here so they get bored and restless. They'll grow out of it and the last thing they need is a criminal record.'

Jane's latent anger erupted. 'They should've thought about that before they dragged Nick into their nasty little scheme.'

'I hardly think he needed "dragging".' The doctor smirked. 'According to our sons he was the instigator.'

'Oh, I see the way it goes. The two of you have ganged up to make sure my brother gets the blame. Typical. Money talks every time.' She grabbed Nick's arm. 'Come on, we're going. We're wasting our time here.'

'Jane, please,' Tim pleaded. 'I promise you the three boys will be treated equally. They'll either all be prosecuted or none of them.' He glanced around. 'I'll be in touch with you all after the meeting.'

'Do you have any idea what time that might be?' Jane asked.

'Not really, my dear. We're starting at two o'clock but

I suspect this might be quite … a contentious discussion because there are fourteen of us, including myself, with wildly varying points of view.'

'We're off.' Dr Menear hauled his son from the room with the Hoopers following close behind.

'Are you goin' into work today?' Hal asked as the three of them walked out together.

'Yes, after lunch.' She struggled to smile. 'Although I'll probably mess up the till receipts and stack the peas where the carrots should be.'

'Freshlands will survive. Does Nick need to get to school?'

'He's missed the bus and by the time he gets the next regular one it won't be worth going.'

'How about I drop you off back at your place and run him on down to Truro?'

'Whatever.' Nick shrugged.

They were a grim, silent group driving out of the village. Jane rushed straight into the kitchen to find her mother sitting at the table with a cold cup of coffee in front of her. After she explained how they'd got on Val was oddly quiet. 'Aren't you supposed to be working today?' Jane asked 'I can drop you off on my way.'

'I was.' Her mother's face crumpled. 'Jenny rang and said she thought it was best if I … took a little break until all this upset with Nick is sorted out. People are …'

'… talking? What a surprise. This is Little Penhaven after all.' Anger surged through her. 'Get your coat and bag. We're leaving in five minutes. You've done nothing wrong.'

'But—'

'—but nothing, Mum. I'm popping to the loo a minute, then we're off.'

A short while later her confidence plummeted when everyone stopped talking as they walked into the crowded shop. Everyone that is apart from a red-faced Colonel Vyvyan, busy declaring his views on her brother and his partners in crime in a voice more suited to the parade ground.

'Bloody yobs. Bring back National Service I say. A year in the forces would soon knock a bit of sense into them.'

It took all of Jane's self-restraint not to ask the obnoxious man how that had worked out for his son. Everyone knew he'd forced the shy, self-effacing Grenville Vyvyan into his old regiment with disastrous results. Grenville had led a training exercise on Bodmin Moor during which a recruit died and, although an investigation couldn't prove or disprove negligence on his part, he'd lost his fellow soldiers' confidence and was allowed to quietly resign. The last Jane heard he'd been shunted off to work on a sheep farm in Australia.

'Colonel, do you think I might I have a word?' Tim Farnham's appearance stirred a number of pointed looks and no one rushed to leave the shop. They weren't missing a good showdown. 'It might be wiser to reserve our discussion on this subject for the PCC meeting.'

'You might not care to hear my opinion, vicar, but I've got every right to express it. There are some of us in this village who choose to uphold good moral standards whether or not that's politically expedient in today's society. You'll have your work cut out to convince the council that those louts shouldn't be prosecuted.' Vyvyan gave a curt nod and blustered out of the shop.

'He doesn't speak for everyone.' Jenny Pascoe's firm tone took Jane by surprise, although it shouldn't have done. 'Not that any of us condone what the boys did.'

'I wouldn't expect you to. We certainly don't,' said Jane quickly.

'But fair's fair. Your Nick's a good boy who did one daft thing, but haven't we all at some time or another? The other pair ... well maybe old Colonel Blimp's got the right idea there.' She chuckled. 'You run along to work. I'll see your mum's all right.'

'Thanks.'

'I'm sorry about that, my dear.' Tim walked outside with her.

'It's not your fault. I hope the rest of the council are more ...'

'... compassionate? We're a mixture as it should be but don't lose heart. I've been doing a little quiet canvassing. I know Cynthia Bullen will definitely vote alongside me.'

'Mrs Bullen?' Jane would have placed the no-nonsense woman firmly on the side of coming down hard on young troublemakers.

'She's a kind soul underneath all that, shall we say, resoluteness?' Tim's eyes twinkled. 'Cynthia believes in giving people a second chance. Remember she stood up for young Mr Day before anyone else.'

'And the others?'

'I'm sure Mrs Halsey will side with the Colonel. Virginia considers herself a ... moral arbiter shall we say?'

She didn't dislike many people but the over-perfumed, full-of-herself London transplant made the top of Jane's short list. She'd imbued one of her new characters with

77

traces of the woman's haughty manner and clichéd taste in the suitable clothes for country life, and she was on track to meet a grisly end later in the story.

'I'm sure we can rely on the charming Fliss to stand up for Christian charity.'

'Fliss is on the PCC?'

'Oh yes. An amazing young woman indeed.' Farnham beamed. 'I don't know where she finds the time, but she never misses a meeting. This village gained a huge asset when young Jory married her.' He looked thoughtful. 'I would say the rest of the council are more on the fence and could be swayed either way.'

'Thanks for everything you're doing. Whichever way things go we won't forget how supportive you've been.'

'I was a teenage boy too once.'

'Yes, but I'm sure you never did anything like this.'

'Now Jane, you're old enough to know we all have our secrets and regrets.' He cracked a rueful smile. 'At fifteen I rarely went to church unless my parents dragged me there and my mother could tell you stories that would make your hair curl. The idea that I'd become a vicar would have made her and everyone who knew me in those days roar with laughter.' Tim patted her shoulder. 'Keep the faith.'

She nodded, blinked back a rush of hot tears and scurried away.

'You're the stubbornest woman I ever met.' Cadan stormed out of the kitchen past Hal.

'What've you done to rile your poor husband this time?'

Sam glowered at him from her seat at the table and

continued stirring her tea with a fury that made him sorry for the spoon.

'He's the stubborn one.'

'Yeah of course 'cos stubbornness definitely doesn't run through the Muir family. We're testament to that,' said Hal.

'I might've guessed you'd be on his side.'

Hal held his arms in the air. 'Don't take it out on me. I don't have a clue what's goin' on. I thought you two were lovebirds again?'

Sam scoffed.

'Come on, you might as well tell me.' He dragged out a chair and flopped down. The plate of mince pies in the middle of the table tempted him so he gave in and took one. After driving Nick into Truro he'd skipped lunch and taken advantage of the mild, dry weather to fit in a decent ten-mile run.

'Obviously there's somethin' wrong with me wanting to make improvements to the house. It's not my fault the plumbing is out of the Dark Ages.'

'You promised you wouldn't climb on any ladders or—'

'—I didn't … well, not really.' Sam looked furious. 'It was only a couple of steps …'

Hal itched to shake her. She couldn't seem to get it through her thick skull how worried her husband was. Sharing their fears didn't mean they'd disappeared.

'I know I shouldn't have.' She exhaled a deep sigh. 'And yeah he has every right to be concerned.'

'But?'

'All this inactivity is driving me crazy. I feel my body

doesn't belong to me any more.' Sam rested her head on the table and burst into tears.

Hal shifted his chair closer and patted her shoulder. Crying women freaked him out but a tearful, pregnant one? That was a whole other ball game.

'Don't fret. It's only baby hormones.' She straightened back up and wiped her red, swollen eyes. 'I'll put my big girl panties on, go find Cadan and prostrate myself at his feet.' Sam gave a hoarse laugh. 'Oh yeah, can't do that or I'll never get up again without a winch.'

'Just for the record, what were you doing anyway?'

'Fixin' your shower.' The gleam returned to her eyes. 'Works pretty damn good now if I say it myself.'

'I'm sure it does. Changing the subject, are you up to speed on Jane's brother?'

'No, but I want to know.' Her gaze narrowed. 'Fix me a coffee. A regular one not that weak decaf crap. I'm allowed one a day and I'm claimin' it now. Tell me all about Nick and then I expect to hear about Kristen Weeks.'

Hal groaned. 'Family grapevine?'

'Yep. Does Jane know?'

'No, but I'll tell her when the timing's right.'

'Don't leave it too long. It won't look good for you if she finds out by herself.'

*Tell me something I don't already know*, Hal thought to himself.

# Chapter Eleven

How much longer would they have to wait? Everyone was pretending to stay busy as if they weren't waiting for the phone to ring. Her mother was limping around the house with the spray polish and a duster. Nick was pretending to do his homework at the kitchen table. And her? Jane had changed out of her Freshlands uniform and tried to write before giving that up as a bad job when she couldn't concentrate and scrubbed the bathroom instead.

'Was that a car stopping outside?'

'I'll check.' Nick walked over to the front door as someone rang the bell. 'It's the vicar.' Panic laced his voice. 'I thought he was going to phone? Why has he come to see us? It's got to be bad news.'

'How about letting him in so we can find out?' Jane's heart thumped. 'Come in, vicar.'

'Thank you my dear. Ah, there you are Nick. Is your mum around?'

'I'll get her, she's—'

'—I'm here. Hello, vicar.' Every line of her mother's body radiated stress and Jane felt for her.

'I feel like the angel bringing tidings of great joy to the shepherds today.' He beamed. 'The council voted not to pursue prosecution on the vandalism charges. The vote was deadlocked and Cynthia Bullen broke the tie.'

'That's wonderful.' Jane couldn't stop smiling. 'We'll be sure to thank her later.'

'I'm sorry. Really sorry,' Nick mumbled.

'I know you are, my boy.'

'We can't give you money like the others did but I'd like to do something to put things right,' he added.

She'd never been prouder of her brother.

'You're a good lad. The others boys haven't offered but our refurbishment fund has benefited greatly so it's not my place to judge them.' Tim sighed. 'We'll leave that to a higher authority but even so … it would be a huge help if you cleaned the graffiti off the door, and I understand you're good with computers?'

'Yeah, I suppose.'

'The church website needs updating. Could you do that?'

'No problem.'

'I've got one condition.' Jane's interruption made everyone stare. 'I'd love you to join us in the Queen's Head tonight, vicar. I'm one of six finalists in a national crime writing competition and my friends have organised a party.' She swallowed down a rush of tears. 'Without this amazing news, I wouldn't have felt like celebrating.'

'I'd be honoured.' Tim winked. 'Plus, I'm afraid if I say no you'll kill me off in your next book. Vicars make frequent fodder for British mystery writers.'

'I'm sure she'll toss in a delinquent teenage victim soon,' Nick joked.

Jane gave in to her impulse to hug him and for once he didn't push her away. Life was looking up.

Hal hovered near the church gate and hoped he'd spot Jane and her family arriving at the pub. He'd agreed to meet her inside but that would mean running the gauntlet of her curious friends alone. The pub looked more enticing tonight with sparkling white Christmas lights draped over the granite facade and evergreen wreaths decorated with red bows hanging in every window. A pang of memory sliced through him. Yesterday had been the second of December his father's birthday, which meant that today his parents would put up all their Christmas decorations. They'd continued the tradition started by Hal's grandparents of waiting until then in an effort to make their son's birthday special before the festive chaos started.

In California he'd hired a professional decorator to take care of his Malibu estate because he always used to host a large party for his clients and business acquaintances between Christmas and New Year. The decoration was as much part of the planning as the food and drink to be served. Each year had a theme and tasteful colour scheme, worlds away from the mismatch of ornaments and decorations his parents had collected over nearly forty years of marriage.

'You goin' to stand there all night?'

His cousin's breezy voice took him by surprise. He hadn't spotted Sam and Cadan heading out from the car park. 'Oh hi, I was just thinkin' of you ... well your family.' Hal pointed to the pub. 'Not up to your folks' standards.'

'I've learned that the Brits don't go for outdoor decorations as much.' She grinned at her husband. 'Probably because the weather's usually too crappy to be out hangin' it all up.'

'Maybe we've got more taste,' Cadan joked.

'Hey, you're the one who climbed all over Gweal Day to put ours up before Hal arrived.'

'Only to stop you doing it.'

'Let's quit there. I don't want to stir up marital disharmony twice in one day,' Hal cut in.

'At least it makes life interesting.' Cadan chuckled.

'That's not what you said about the shower.'

'Time out, kids.' Hal glanced at the church clock. 'I'd better go on in or Jane will wonder where I've got to.'

'Oh boy, he's got it bad.' Sam laughed and then started to wave frantically. 'Hey Jane, your boyfriend's here and pining for you.'

'You're a pest,' he muttered. 'You were as a kid and you haven't changed a scrap.'

'Neither have you. You were a cocky little—'

'—stop it you two,' Cadan complained. 'You're worse than me and Jory.'

Sam rolled her eyes. 'That is so not true.' She jabbed Hal's arm. 'Go on with you. Jane deserves a bit of fun and, for some unknown reason, she's got the hots for you. No accounting for taste.' Her smile lost some of its brightness. 'But if you hurt her—'

'—I'll have you and the rest of the SAPs to deal with. Yeah, I get it.' Hal popped a kiss on her cheek. 'See you later. I'll leave you and your poor husband to make your way over to the pub at slow pregnant lady pace.'

She could absolutely handle being swept off her feet any time by Hal. The heady sensation of being wrapped up in warm, delectable male gorgeousness was better than being shortlisted in any competition. She ignored her mum's blatant stare and laughed at Nick's grimace. Teenagers were typically revolted if anyone they considered to be ancient behaved as if they weren't completely past it. Jane hadn't reached her sell-by date quite yet.

He looked slightly sheepish when he set her back down. 'We're gonna spend some time alone later if I have to kidnap you.'

'It's only kidnapping if the "victim" isn't willing.' She giggled. 'At least that's the way it works in my books.'

'Are we going inside or not? I'm starved,' Nick complained. 'We didn't have any tea.'

'You put away a whole box of mince pies when you got home from college.'

'I'm a growing boy.'

'I'm in agreement with you Nick, because I'm famished too,' Hal said. 'Sam put us on rations as well at Gweal Day. How are you doin' Mrs Davy?'

His kindness to her mother touched Jane. She'd jumped to completely erroneous conclusions about him the first time she saw his photo. Well, not completely. The photograph hadn't done justice to how seriously gorgeous he was in person.

'I'm all right thanks, but I'm getting cold standing out here.'

'Sorry, Mum. Let's get in and warm up.'

The moment they entered the pub Fliss rushed out to greet them, looking as though she'd stepped off the front cover of a fashion magazine instead of out from a hot kitchen. She'd probably been on her feet for hours but her chef's whites were immaculate, her make-up remained camera-worthy and not a strand of her elegant blonde hair was out of place.

'There you are. I'll have the champagne brought in now

you're here.' Her blue eyes shone. 'I didn't dare to take it in before or your friends would've drunk the lot!'

'Never.'

'John Pickering warned us about the SAPs before we took over the pub. I believe "make bloody sure you get in extra chardonnay when they're coming" is how he phrased it.' Fliss's posh accent, courtesy of her expensive education and wealthy parents, stood out here but no one could deny how hard she'd worked to fit in. 'I've got trays of appetisers ready to pass around and the main course will be ready in about half an hour.'

'Perfect. These men are begging to be fed.'

'Oh, men are always begging. The trick is to make them wait just long enough,' Fliss trilled and disappeared through to the kitchen.

'Sheesh, she's somethin' else.' Hal whistled. 'That's one smart cookie.'

Jane pulled him close and lowered her voice. 'You won't say that when I make you wait later.'

'You won't either.' He slid his hand down to her waist. 'Works both ways. Let's go get this party started.'

# Chapter Twelve

Hal's assumption that English people were quiet and reserved flew out of the window when the noise level at the party rose to resemble a Muir family gathering. He savoured every moment of watching Jane enjoy the limelight for a change.

'You get an A-plus for surviving your first run-in with the SAPs.' Jane returned from the kitchen brandishing two mugs. 'Your reward is a good cup of coffee.' Luckily her mum was kind enough to go straight to bed when they got back and dragged a reluctant Nick upstairs too.

'That's kind of you, but I was hoping for somethin' a little more ... interesting.' He prised the mugs from her hands and set them on the table. 'First off, how about tellin' me if I passed muster with your girlfriends?' There'd been enough whispered conversations and blatant stares his way to know he'd been a prime subject for discussion. Hal slid his arms around her waist and pulled her close.

'As you might guess you rated a ten out of ten for, shall we say, your physical appearance. They adored your accent and are big fans of the way you treat me.' A frown nestled between her eyes. 'Overall, I'd say you scored an eight out of ten.'

'Oh yeah. What'd they mark me down on?' He saw her expression change. 'The fact no one knows how long I'm staying, what my plans are next and whether you're simply a holiday romance as far as I'm concerned?' She nodded and buried her face in his chest. 'Look at me, Jane.'

'Oh, Hal.' Her luminous blue eyes shimmered with

tears. 'It's been such a beautiful night and I can't bear to have it spoiled. Would you mind lying for once? Please.'

'Why would I need to do that?'

'Because we both know—'

'—stop right there.' He refused to take the coward's way out. 'We don't "know" anythin' because we've never really talked about it. About us.'

'Is there an "us"?'

The fact she asked that particular question disappointed him.

'Sorry. I didn't phrase that well. For a writer I'm not always great with words.'

Hal's hands dropped away. 'Let's sit, drink our coffee and hash this out.'

*What was the saying about being careful what you asked for?* If she hadn't opened her big mouth Hal would've whisked her off somewhere to do things she'd only ever fantasised about. Instead she got Freshlands instant coffee and her dreams shattered. 'I suppose you'd better get on with it.'

'We're not goin' to our execution.'

'Feels a bit like it,' she muttered.

'When I asked Sam if I could come and stay in the first place I only mentioned staying for a couple of weeks.'

'Oh.' Jane bit her lip hard enough to taste blood.

'Don't panic. They're not in a hurry to throw me out, and I'm not in a rush to go. In fact Sam's threatened me if I dare to leave before Christmas.'

'So, twenty more days give or take?' She struggled to keep her voice steady.

'I'm thinkin' about what to do next work-wise but haven't settled on anything definite yet.'

'But how will you manage for money?' Hal's gaze turned wary and she wanted to smack herself. 'Am I the only one who doesn't know?'

'Know what?'

Lisa and Pat had asked probing questions earlier while Heather flat-out asked whether she'd checked Hal's online presence. Now it all clicked. They'd poked around on her behalf and been shocked at the results.

'Oh God, you're rolling in it, aren't you?' She covered her face with her hands. 'Now everyone will say I'm after you for your money.'

'Your friends would never do that and other people ... do they matter?'

'You're not denying it?'

'No. I'm not Bill Gates but I co-owned a very successful business. I sold that and my large house. The money's invested well and I don't need to rush into getting another job.'

'You don't need to work again if you don't want to?' Wrapping her head around that idea was close to impossible.

'If I say it's only money, you'll call me an unthinkin' bastard but if I lie, you'll hate me.' Hal shrugged. 'It's a no-win situation where I'm concerned, sweetheart. Can you see me sittin' around and doing nothing?'

'No.'

'So, are we good about that part?'

'I suppose.'

'Do you want to move on to talking about the holiday

romance bit? I'm gettin' the impression it won't make much difference because you've made your decision already.'

'Why would you say that?'

'Because you're looking at us like one of your plots. You've told me how you plot the story out chapter by chapter all the way through to the ending before you start to write.' There was a new raspy edge to his voice. 'I'm not gonna pretend I've been a saint, but I've always been straightforward with women and, with a couple of exceptions, most of my girlfriends appreciated it.' His sharp burst of laughter ebbed away. 'I've never been engaged or married, and my only quasi-serious relationship ended when I asked my ex, Lanie, to move in with me a few years ago. She'd apparently expected a proposal, so we parted ways.' The corners of his mouth twitched in a fleeting smile. 'In case you're interested, I've never told any woman I loved her.'

'Not even …?'

'Nope, not even Lanie.' Hal's steady gaze rested on her. 'You're different than any of them. I'm different with you.'

'Is that good or bad?'

'What do you think?' His voice was rough with emotion and tore her apart.

'Good. What we have is good.'

'Yeah, I thought so too until the dissection started.' Now his eyes softened. 'I'm pretty sure you're gonna break my record.'

Heat flooded through her. 'Really?'

'Why do you find that so hard to believe?' Hal shook his head. 'I can't do this any longer.'

'What?' Jane's heart raced.

Hal scooped her up and plonked her unceremoniously on his knees. 'The cardinal rule of serious conversation is no physical contact,' he said. 'But with you smelling wonderful and almost close enough to taste you're bloody distracting me beyond all hope of talking sense.'

A hint of devilment crept into her soft blue eyes. He traced the contours of her face, loving when she shivered into his stroking fingers. His body tightened, imagining exploring every inch of her as she responded to his fervent kiss.

Jane wriggled her hands up under his jumper and grinned when she discovered bare skin. 'You're always so ... warm.'

'That's because of you.' Her face took on a rosy glow. 'My turn.' He took his time unbuttoning the row of miniscule pearl buttons holding her dark red and cream blouse together. She wouldn't appreciate him ripping it open. 'If these were designed to slow a man down they did the trick, but I'm not easily defeated.'

'Good.' Jane's laugh filled the room. 'You still don't get the black lace because I didn't expect ...'

'To be ravished in your own home?' Hal's words made her smile disappear, reminding her that her family were upstairs. He pulled the edges of her blouse together and brushed a gentle kiss over her mouth. 'When do you next have three or four days off work?'

'Three or four? You must be joking. Everyone is doing overtime between now and Christmas whether they want to or not.' Jane grimaced. 'It'll be torture. Non-stop

Christmas music, increasingly bad-tempered customers and an impending shortage of chipolata sausages. I can't complain too much because the extra money will be handy.'

He brushed a lock of hair from her face, wishing like anything he could offer to make up the difference in pay for the opportunity to have her to himself sooner. 'So, when can the handsome prince whisk Cinderella away from everything?'

'The longest break I'll have is from around teatime on Sunday the fifteenth until I go in for an afternoon shift on the Tuesday.'

A trickle of uncertainty sneaked in. 'I don't mean to assume ...'

'I want to assume things with you.'

'Good. Tell me what I can do to help you out and save you from gettin' totally exhausted while flogging mince pies to the masses.'

'And you're offering this totally from the goodness of your heart with no ulterior motive involved?'

'I'm wounded you could suggest such a thing.' He dramatically clutched his chest.

'Clearly rubbing shoulders with Hollywood royalty hasn't rubbed off on you. You're a lousy actor.'

'I'll retract my offer if you aren't careful.'

'I won't be the only one suffering if I'm worn out.' Her eyes twinkled. 'My hours don't coincide well with Mum's, so if you could be her taxi service if she's stuck for a lift that would be great.'

'No problem. How's she coping? I thought she looked livelier tonight.'

'She really was. She loves the job. Jenny's a kind soul and the money is a help but far more important is the sense of purpose it's given her. We all need that.'

'We sure do.' He stroked her cheek. 'I don't want to leave but you've got work tomorrow.'

'I don't go in until noon and work until closing time at eight. It's my least favourite shift.'

'How about meeting me for brunch at the pub? Sam told me Fliss fixes the best pancakes outside of the USA.'

'I'd love to. They are pretty good, although I can't comment on their authenticity.'

'That's a date.' Following in his cousin's footsteps, this particular situation was the last thing he expected when he hopped on a plane in Knoxville. It worked out for Sam, so why shouldn't they be equally lucky? The impatient streak that got him into trouble as a teenager occasionally still needed reining in but with Jane's luminous eyes fixed on him and her soft mouth pressed against his, Hal struggled to remember why impulsive decisions were often a bad idea.

# Chapter Thirteen

Jane screwed up the paper bag with the remains of her pasty and resolutely tossed it in the bin. In her heart she knew it was ridiculous to believe that either eating or not eating the last couple of bites would make any difference to how the sexy black lace underwear fitted. A trickle of nerves pooled at the pit of her stomach. Hal was super fit and had worked with some of the world's most beautiful women. Would he have expectations she couldn't live up to?

*This is Hal you're talking about*, she said to herself. *The man who's happily run your mum to and from work this week. Helped your teenage brother scrub graffiti off the church door. Brought you homemade soup when you were too tired to cook after being on your feet for eight hours – well, homemade by Sam, but that's just nitpicking.*

The few slivers of memory of her father had almost disappeared by now, meaning her first-hand knowledge of how men treat the women they're supposed to love had been shaped by Ralph Davy. Realistically, she knew he didn't represent all men and there were plenty of positive examples around her to refute it. Sam and Cadan. Heather and Mole. Kate and Timothy. Three wildly different couples who showed nothing but love and respect for each other.

She checked the time. Only another two hours to survive. When she returned to work on Tuesday afternoon, they'd only have a fortnight to go until they shut the doors on Christmas Eve. She refused to think about the post-Boxing Day sales.

'Caught you clock watching,' Philip teased. 'Is the tea stewed?'

'Probably. I had coffee instead.' Jane glanced at the door, wishing someone else would join them in the break room. She'd avoided being on her own with Philip since their lunch date although he'd cornered her a few times in the shop with various offers, all of which she'd refused.

When she was stocking shelves she'd learned to keep one eye on Philip and dart around the next aisle if she saw him heading her way. Being on cashier duty was easier because he couldn't commandeer her for a private conversation there.

'I need to get back to work.'

'You've another ten minutes yet.' He dragged out a chair and opened his plastic lunch box. 'It's Sunday so it must be ...' Philip lifted out a sandwich.

'Cheese and pickle.' Jane laughingly finished his sentence. His widowed mother was nothing if not predictable. Despite the fact Philip had moved out into his own flat several years ago Eileen Bunt still insisted that he stopped by to see her every day and always had a packed lunch ready for him. The sharp-tongued woman had regarded Jane with massive suspicion the one time Philip took her home with him for Sunday tea. Mrs Bunt had high expectations for her only child and made it clear Jane didn't fit her plan.

'Tomorrow will be roast beef left from today's dinner.' He rattled off the rest of the week's offerings with good humour but suddenly his demeanour altered and he seized her wrist.

'What are you doing? Let go of me.'

'Answer one question and I will.'

'What is it?'

'Tell me what on earth you can possibly have in common with that slick Yank?'

Hal would tear Philip off a strip for daring to call him a Yank before he ripped him apart for daring to lay a finger on her.

'He's not like us, Jane.' His voice roughened. 'What has Muir told you about his life out there in Hollywood? Does the name Kristen Weeks mean anything to you?'

Not answering seemed her smartest move.

'You ought to ask him how she died. No wonder he bailed out of his gym business and crawled over here with his tail between his legs,' Philip scoffed. 'You and I are alike. We get on well and could make a great life together. I love you. I've always loved you.'

'Don't say—'

'—oh there you are, Mr Bunt.' Mandy Johnson burst in, red-faced and flustered.

Jane could have kissed the cashier.

'Sorry to interrupt your lunch but we need you out there. Two women are fighting over the last *Star Wars* selection box. Poor Jimmy tried to break them up but one of them slugged him. He'll have a right old shiner tomorrow.'

She suppressed the urge to get out her notebook but would remember to jot it down later. Hal had joked the other day that he ought to warn people when they were out together that anything they said or did could end up in one of her books.

'I'm coming.' He tossed his uneaten sandwich away and tucked the lunch box under his arm.

She'd push what he'd told her about Hal to the back of her mind for now and deal with it another day.

'Family three-line whip tonight.' Sam breezed into the kitchen as much as a nearly eight months pregnant lady could "breeze" anywhere. 'Jory and Fliss are kicking off their "Countdown to Christmas" festivities with a quiz.'

Before Hal could protest his cousin stared him into silence.

'Yeah, Jane knows because I just texted to her. It's teams of four and we're gonna be the Gweal Day Geniuses.'

*Thanks a bunch.* So much for the quiet evening he'd planned before their romantic getaway tomorrow. Sam was already cross with him because he refused to divulge any details, but he hadn't trusted her not to blab to the rest of the SAPs. The last thing he needed was input from the five women. Cadan was different. The more he got to know him, the more he enjoyed the quiet Cornishman's company. On several evenings this week they'd retreated to his shed and Hal worked on a surprise for Jane while Cadan put the finishing touches to Sam's desk. They always wrapped up with a beer and swopped confidences they knew stayed within the four wooden walls.

'I'm useless at quizzes.'

'You're not as dumb as you make out,' Sam scoffed. 'Plus you're our eye candy to distract the other players.'

'What about me?' Cadan pretended to be offended.

'You're my personal eye candy and I'm not sharin' you. Jane will have to suck one up for the team.' She winked at Hal. 'You'll make it up to her tomorrow, I'm sure.'

Sometimes silence was the best answer.

'We're leavin' at half past six. Be ready.' Sam stomped out of the room.

'You think havin' a baby's gonna slow her down?'

'Not for long. My lady doesn't do slow. Well ...' Cadan cleared his throat.

'Best leave it there, mate,' he warned.

Once he'd showered and changed Hal grabbed his rain jacket and headed back downstairs. This week's weather fitted Jane's description of a typical Cornish winter. If he took the weather forecasters' numbers to heart the temperatures really weren't that cold, but the gloomy skies and steady drizzle helped to give a different impression. Sam laughed in his face one day when he complained about it.

'Sorry to break the news but if you stay long enough, you'll get used to it,' she'd said. 'It's grown on me. I about boiled to death when we were back in Knoxville in early July. My skin's never been better and I even find myself agreein' when people say that the rain is good for the gardens.'

'I'm gonna walk if you two don't mind.' Although he was going for a run most mornings the lack of constant activity didn't suit him. He'd made a quick phone call to Jane and they'd light-heartedly bemoaned the fact they wouldn't get a chance to sneak a few minutes alone tonight because her mother was coming along and Val had dragooned Nick into joining them.

'You'll get soaked.'

'Tell me somethin' I don't know.' Hal laughed off Cadan's warning. 'I reckon you could wring out most Cornish people this time of year and get enough rainwater to fill a reservoir.'

Thankfully there was a slight break in the weather and only the bottom hem of his jeans and his shoes were damp when he reached the village. Little Penhaven was growing on him too. He'd visited a couple of the so-called prettier spots around Cornwall this week and, even though it was winter-time and many of the shops and attractions were closed, he could see why they appealed to so many tourists. Back in Los Angeles he avoided the hot-spots too whenever possible, preferring to venture further north to Monterey and Carmel or explore lesser known spots in the San Gabriel Mountains. Similarly, when he was home in Knoxville he avoided Gatlinburg and Pigeon Forge at all costs.

Hal strolled past Jenny Pascoe's shop and the post office before catching a whiff of beef chop suey from the Chinese restaurant Sam had warned him to avoid. He stopped to admire the floodlit church. It never ceased to amaze him to discover such architecturally stunning buildings in small communities with relatively few inhabitants to support them. Talk about a leap of faith.

'Waiting for someone?'

He was surrounded by hints of tropical fruit as a surprising kiss from Jane landed on his mouth. 'You. Always.' He swept her into a tight hug. 'I mean it.' Hal's whispered declaration made her cheek burn against his own.

'Save that.' She smiled and let go of him. 'Are you ready to destroy the competition?'

'My only hope is to survive this without humiliating myself or you too badly. I bet you're a quiz expert?'

'Hardly. The SAPs have entered a few at other pubs around here but only for fun.'

'She's being modest as usual.' Val bragged on her daughter. 'Nine times out of ten they win and my girl's the main reason. If they weren't split up in different teams tonight, they'd be sure to win the Christmas dinner. It's a goose from a local farm with all the trimmings.'

'Ignore her. She's my mum so she's got to exaggerate my brilliance.' Jane brushed it off.

'We'll see. Come on.' Hal linked his arm through hers.

A wave of noise hit him in the face. The quiz didn't start for another half an hour but the pub was already wall to wall people.

'Over here, mate.' Cadan waved from a corner at the back of the large rectangular room. 'Perks of knowing the landlord. He saved us this big table.'

'I'll get the drinks in,' Hal offered. 'What do y'all want?'

'I love hearing the south come out in your accent.' Sam laughed. 'I'm glad they didn't completely knock it out of you in La-La Land.'

Her remark struck him hard. For years he'd largely left Tennessee and all it represented behind, seeing that as the only way to move on from his rebellious days. But now Hal was having a major rethink. Since living at Gweal Day and getting involved with Jane he'd become aware of the more positive effects of family and community. The few friends he'd made in Los Angeles were mostly connected with work and he doubted any of them would lose a minute's sleep over him. It wasn't how he wanted to live the rest of his life.

'You getting those drinks or are we going to die of thirst?' Cadan chided. 'Save the few decent brain cells you've got for the quiz. Come on. I'll give you a hand.'

'Did you get bloody roped in to uphold the Day family honour?' Jory teased Hal and started pulling a pint while he listened to the rest of their order. Despite his radical lifestyle change, he still looked more quintessential surfer than pub landlord.

'I think I'm just included to make up the numbers.'

'You'd better not be. I'll get Jane's wine.'

'He's making a good job of this place. I had my doubts, but Sam was right… again. Fliss has been the making of my brother.' Cadan cocked a sardonic smile at Jory. 'The right woman usually sorts us out. Isn't that so, little brother?'

'Most of the time this moron talks shit, but in this case … I'll defer to his wisdom.'

'Chalk that one up.'

'If I wouldn't lose my tenancy, I'd punch you.' Jory's threat came with a massive grin. 'Now clear off. Some of us have work to do.'

Hal picked up the tray of drinks. 'Something tells me you're not a quiz fan either, Cadan?'

'You've got to be kidding. My plan is to sit tight and let the women do all the work then take the credit later.'

'As if Sam will let you get away with that.'

'Get away with what?'

Trust his cousin to have excellent hearing.

'Nothing, my love.' Cadan swooped in for a kiss but she grabbed him by the shirt collar.

''fess up now or you'll be in even bigger trouble.'

'We were jokin' around that's all.' Hal rattled off their plan. 'Just acknowledging you're smarter than us.'

Sam wagged a finger at Jane. 'You'd better watch out, he's a smooth talker.'

*Not helpful*, Hal thought.

'Oh, I've got the measure of him. Don't worry.'

Instead of the scepticism he'd expected, Jane sounded amused. Hal snagged the chair next to her, draped his arm around her shoulder and gave his cousin a satisfied nod.

'Listen up everyone.' Jory rang the large brass bell hanging over the bar. 'You all know the rules. Turn your phones off and stick them in the middle of your table. My sweet wife will walk around to check no one's cheating and trust me you don't want to piss her off. I've done it before and it doesn't end well.' Everyone laughed and Fliss tossed him a fake glare. 'One person writes down the answers for the team and we'll collect them after each round.' He gestured to Nick. 'He's my runner tonight.'

'Off we go. Let's find out the topic for the first round.' Jory pulled a piece of paper out of a red plastic bucket. 'Sport.'

The faintest chance of not making a complete fool of himself rose a notch or two.

# Chapter Fourteen

'Wow, we should crown you two the Queen and King of pub quizzes.' Sam lifted her glass of orange juice. 'A toast to our resident geniuses. Talk about Anglo-American cooperation at its finest.'

A hot flush crept up Jane's neck and Hal's embarrassment matched her own. She shouldn't have been surprised when he rattled off the answers to a broad range of questions from football to Greek mythology. The man had more layers to him than puff pastry.

'Val, we've all agreed that you can have the Christmas dinner prize because I've already got a huge turkey on order from Tom Pendeen.' Sam wouldn't listen to her mother's protests. 'I guess Hal gets to choose which he prefers to eat on December twenty-fifth. My bet's on the goose.'

She shouldn't be so ridiculously flustered at her age but, with tomorrow on her mind and a lingering juvenile excitement from the Gweal Day Geniuses' success at wiping the floor with the competition, Jane's emotions were all over the place.

'It's okay,' Hal whispered. 'You know I'll always pick you … goose or turkey. Makes no difference as long as you're there.'

'For goodness sake, get a room.' Sam guffawed. 'Oh. that's right, you've got—'

'—quit it, cuz. Doesn't matter to me but Jane's a bit sensitive.'

'All right if I hang on to help clear glasses?' Nick reappeared, looking flushed and happier than she'd seen in a while. 'Jory's really swamped, John Pickering's off home soon and Fliss needs to take care of Kit.'

Jane only just managed to stop herself from replying one way or the other. 'You'd better ask Mum.'

'Oh yeah, right.'

'Good call.' Hal squeezed her hand. 'It's a hard habit to break.'

'Most bad ones are.'

'Tell me about it.'

'No, you'll tell me tomorrow.' His brow furrowed. Jane guessed his timetable for their getaway ran more along the lines of baring his body than his soul. He'd discover she wanted both.

'All sorted.' Nick tapped her shoulder. 'Mum wasn't keen on me walking home late, but it's okay because Jory offered for me to crash here for the night.'

'You'll be up in time for the school bus?' Jane shrugged an apology. 'Sorry, I'm not supposed to—'

'—it's okay. I will. Promise.' Nick shuffled his feet. 'Have a good time with Hal. You deserve it and he's okay. I'll see you again Tuesday.'

He was far from being a little kid so why did it feel awkward to have her brother wishing her well?

'Got to grow up sometime, Jane,' Nick said with a smile.

'Me or you?'

'Both of us.'

'Smart boy,' Hal conceded.

'It's time I took my lady home before she falls asleep in my beer,' Cadan announced. 'You want a ride, mate?'

'Yeah, if it's okay with mine?' He threw a panicked glance Jane's way. 'I didn't mean ... well I did ...'

'Shush. Go home and I'll work on winkling Mum out of here,' Jane said. 'I'll see you in the morning. We'll ... talk then.'

'Talk, yeah we sure will.' Hal's earnestness made it almost impossible not to laugh. His long, possessive kiss set off a raucous round of cheers around the pub. With most people well into the Christmas spirit by now the "encouraging" remarks they yelled out would have made a sailor blush. She reluctantly broke away and found Val.

'Are you ready, Mum?'

'Whenever you are.'

*Oh, I am so ready.*

He'd batted various ideas back and forth with Cadan before he settled on booking himself and Jane into The Cornwall Estate and Spa halfway between Little Penhaven and Mevagissey. It should fulfil all of his criteria according to Cadan's enthusiastic description.

'Sam lapped it up. We went for a couple of nights to celebrate her birthday,' he'd said. 'She talked me into joining her in the spa treatments. My down to earth father would've killed himself laughing to see me getting a manicure, but the couples' massage converted me to the benefits shall we say?'

The estate wasn't far away so they wouldn't waste too much time travelling. Cadan assured him the rooms were elegant but not fussy and the service responsive but not intrusive. The weather probably wouldn't be much for exploring the extensive grounds, but Hal felt sure they'd find ways to amuse themselves.

The ten minute drive from Gweal Day to Jane's house wasn't long enough to settle the butterflies vying for space in his stomach. A million questions ran through his head from whether she was equally nervous to his overwhelming fear of not living up to her expectations.

*Remember this is Jane. The same Jane you laugh with all the time. The gentle, soft-spoken woman who's found her way into your heart. She says you're kind, clever and handsome – which she puts last on purpose because it's the least important in her eyes.*

'All set?' he asked when she opened the door, determined not to comment on the dark circles under her eyes. She clearly got as much sleep as he did last night.

'Do I have to wear a blindfold?'

Hal considered cracking a joke about not being into that sort of thing but wasn't sure she'd appreciate it.

'I'm aware your name's not Christian Grey.' Now her eyes shone. 'Thank goodness.'

One of the nervous knots untangled. 'Is that your only bag?' They bumped heads as he reached for the small black leather case. 'Oh heck, I'm sorry. Are you all right?'

'I'm fine although it's not terribly romantic to try to knock me out. That's the sort of thing I put in my books when I'm plotting to eliminate a character.'

This was more like them. Hal set the case back down and hugged her, relaxing as Jane settled against his chest with a sigh. 'Let's go have a good time. Whatever that involves.' He ploughed on, determined to say his piece. 'The chance to spend thirty-six uninterrupted hours

106

together … that's a gift. Anything else is a bonus, but it's not goin' to make or break how I feel about you.'

'Are you sure?' Her voice trembled. 'What if I don't live up to your expectations?'

'Remember that works both ways.' He watched as confusion flared in her eyes. 'Most of the "supremely confident man" labels people stick on me are concerned with the surface stuff. Underneath I'm a regular guy wonderin' what a woman sees in me and why she'd ever trust me with … herself.'

'Oh Hal.' She slipped her soft hands around his face and smoothed her fingers over his freshly shaved skin. 'I trust you. Absolutely.'

'That's all I need to hear.'

'How did you know?' Hal's bemused expression told Jane this was a wonderful coincidence. She rarely envied her friends but when Sam described her luxury weekend with Cadan at this gorgeous place it'd been hard not to turn a tiny bit green. 'Did Cadan recommend coming here?'

'Yeah, is somethin' wrong?'

'Far from it.' Jane flung her arms around his neck and plastered him with kisses before explaining. Then she took a mental snapshot of the moment. Everything about the day was perfect starting with the weather. For the first time in a week it wasn't raining and soft wintery sunshine bathed the elegant white building. The hotel was the centrepiece of the estate and dated back to the early 1800s when the Coode family bought the estate. She knew all this because she avidly read up on every detail after Sam had told her about the visit. Hal's azure blue eyes matched the clear, cloudless sky and he gazed at her with such intensity it almost sucked her breath away. 'New cologne?'

He looked a bit embarrassed.

'I love it.' Normally he stuck to plain soap, not that she minded because he always smelled wonderful, but the warm hint of sandalwood with another layer of something that reminded Jane of her favourite blackberry crumble made him even more irresistible. If she told him that he'd no doubt order her to add a dollop of cream and fetch a spoon.

'If it's so awesome, why can you hardly stop laughing?'

Her giggles erupted and it took her a while to calm down long enough to explain. 'I've just realised that there's a reason I don't write romance novels.'

'Oh, I don't know.' He tightened his grip around her waist. 'It's workin' on me.' Hal's playful hip roll left her in no doubt. 'I reckon it's time we checked in, don't you?'

Another flutter of nerves came and disappeared again equally fast. 'Definitely.'

While Hal was checking in Jane sneaked a quick look at the Christmas decorations in the marble lobby. The tasteful white lights and elegant bare twigs sparsely decorated with large silver balls bore little resemblance to her mother's eclectic decorating scheme.

Ten minutes later Hal swiped the card for the Clementina Suite and pushed the door open.

'Wow this is seriously gorgeous.' The stunning black and white colour scheme with splashes of dark red surprised her but totally worked with the soaring ceiling, original plasterwork, impressive granite fireplace and massive bay windows.

'No, you're seriously gorgeous. The room is cool and

has a great view.' The casual compliment made her cheeks flame.

'I'm going to have a good poke around ... you don't mind?' She didn't want him thinking he came second to a fancy hotel. 'All of this is a treat for me, but you're the best part.'

'Don't apologise.' His gentle smile reassured her. 'Anythin' that makes you happy is good with me. Take as long as you like.' Hal set their bags on the black velvet sofa, kicked off his shoes, tucked a pillow behind his head and stretched out on the bed.

'I've never seen anything like this for a start.' The ornate, oversized four-poster was crafted of black wrought iron and she ran her hand up one of the twisted posts, shaped to resemble tree branches.

'Don't tell me, you're already imagining one of your characters impaled on the spikes?' She felt herself blushing. 'Makes me feel kinda medieval.' Hal leered, waggled his eyebrows and patted the puffy white duvet. 'Come here, wench.'

'"Take as long as you like" you said.' Jane laughed and went to investigate the bathroom. 'My God, it's massive. We could have a party in here.'

'Was that an invitation?'

Mirrors reached up from the ebony wood double-vanity unit all the way to the ceiling and a massive claw-foot tub dominated the black and white tiled space. *Big enough for two?*

Jane popped her head back around the door. 'Later.'

The husky promise about killed him. Last night it was easy

to reassure Jane that he wouldn't rush into anything, and he still absolutely meant every word, but the effort would be a damn sight more challenging than he'd expected. Hal reined himself in. 'We can study the nymphs and frolicking animals.'

'The frolicking what?'

Hal pointed to the intricate decorative plasterwork on the ceiling. 'I'm surprised the Victorians didn't cover all this over.'

Jane rested one knee on the bed and glanced upwards. 'I see what you mean.' She eased back to sit next to him.

'You might want to take a look at the spa offerings so we can book whatever sessions you fancy. It all comes as part of the pre-Christmas deal I booked.' Only one treatment was normally included but he'd made an agreement with the manager that anything they wanted would be quietly added to the bill for him to settle later. Hal didn't want this special time together to become about money, although he suspected the topic would arise again at some point.

'Sounds good.' Jane reached for his hand and stroked her fingers over his skin. 'Kiss me.'

'Willingly.' Slipping his hands up through her silky hair he exposed her pale neck to his first kisses. 'New perfume. Hints of lime and musk.' He kept things light until her tongue flicked across his teeth and his self-control cracked. Hal pushed her back on the pillow and deepened the kiss, dragging soft appreciative noises from her. Jane's searching hands ran up and down his spine.

'No one's going to interrupt if you undo the buttons today.' She'd worn the same dark red and cream silk blouse that had tempted him the other night.

'Including you?' Hal needed to be sure. Jane's eyes verged on midnight-blue as she nodded. She didn't laugh or tell him to hurry up as he forced his trembling fingers to do their job. Slowly he pushed the material out of the way to reveal a black lace bra, cut low enough to show off her curves and smooth creamy skin. 'Worth the wait.' He eased her out of the blouse and peeled off his own shirt. 'Strip poker without the cards. Your turn.'

Jane shimmied out of her grey trousers and he struggled not to stare at the other half of the black lace equation.

'I shouldn't have eaten that pasty yesterday, should I?'

'What?'

She stumbled over a garbled explanation about worrying how the delicate underwear fitted.

'Don't be ridiculous.' Arousal thickened his voice. 'You're beautiful. Never think that you're not.' Hal leapt from the bed and tugged off his belt and trousers in record time. 'I planned to take things slow the first time if we got to this point and—' he caught his breath '—I still will if that's what you want but ...'

A sultry smile worked its way across her face. 'I'm beginning to think they're right about Americans talking too much.'

He crawled across the bed and straddled her, then he traced a tortuous path over the black lace, making her whole body tremble and arch under his exploring fingers. 'This is all real pretty, but it's served its purpose now.' He reached around to pop the bra open and soon it and the matching thong were history.

'Isn't it my turn to see you in all your glory now?'

'Anything you want.' With his boxers out of the way

Jane's wide-eyed gaze homed in on him. Hal picked up on her nervousness as he reached for the condom he'd brought with him. 'Remember what I said last night?' He touched her cheek. 'Nothing will affect how much I … how much I love you.'

'It's all good then, because I love you too.'

Without hesitation he shifted over her, kissed her full on the mouth and slowly, deliberately sunk into her.

# Chapter Fifteen

Jane eased back into awareness as late afternoon winter shadows filtered in through the sheer white curtains. She needed to use the bathroom but was pinned in place by Hal's heavy warm arm stretched over her stomach. He was basically comatose and taking up most of the bed but gave a few unintelligible grunts when she made her request and shifted enough for her to slide out from under him.

'God, woman, I'm starvin'. Do you know what time it is?'

She slipped back in next to him and toyed with the crisp blond hair matting his broad chest. 'Yes, it's time for someone to stop grouching and find their happy face.'

'Oh, I'm smilin'.' Hal flashed his trademark grin. 'You're in the bed with me.'

'I suspect we've missed lunch and it's too early for dinner, but I spotted a tea tray when we came in with a few packets of biscuits. Will that keep you going?'

'Maybe. Why don't you go and put the kettle on?'

'I bet you never said that before you came to Cornwall.'

'True. My folks would kill themselves laughin'.'

She didn't want to spoil the moment but having the chance for a proper chat was one reason they'd sneaked away from regular life. 'While the kettle boils I want to hear about your family.' Jane hopped out of bed.

'It's not fair to distract me that way and expect a serious conversation.'

'What way?'

'That way.' He traced the exaggerated shape of her curves in the air.

'There's an easy solution.' Hal's T-shirt was the nearest piece of clothing so she tugged in on. She grabbed his abandoned boxers off the floor and tossed them over. 'Much safer around hot drinks anyway.'

'Are you always this sensible?' he grumbled.

'If I was, I wouldn't be here.' Jane plopped down on the bed.

'True. Now … my family. Well you know that Jesse, my dad, is Sam's uncle right?'

'Yes, and you all live in Knoxville.'

'Yeah, but in different directions outside the city. We're a close family.' The light faded in his eyes. 'At least they all are … I haven't been back much since I graduated high school.'

She heard the kettle turn off.

'I told you before that I left for LA when things didn't pan out with football. The full truth is I didn't tell anyone I was going, hitched rides all the way out there and arrived with fifty dollars in my pocket. The first night I got mugged and lost everything.'

'How on earth did you manage?'

'You takin' notes for your next book?' Hal teased. 'I copied all the wannabe actors and got a job waiting tables. That's where I met Gene.'

Jane listened while he told her everything about meeting the man who'd later become his business partner. The two young men discovered a mutual passion for staying fit, pooled their resources to rent a miniscule apartment and even picked up some male modelling jobs to pay the bills.

'Don't laugh.'

'I'd never do that and anyway—' she playfully dragged her gaze over him '—I'm sure you were extremely sought after.'

'We did okay and once we even got offered parts in an … um, adult film.'

'You were a porn star?'

'No!' The last thing he needed was her jumping to the erroneous conclusion that his naked body was plastered all over the internet as "Horny Hal goes to Hawaii" or something equally appalling. 'We turned it down.' He shoved a hand through his messy hair. 'Why don't you make us those drinks?' Jane gave him a searching look but slid off the bed without arguing. Putting a physical distance between them made it easier to launch into the story of his business, pretty straightforward at first but less so when he tried to explain his gradual disillusionment. 'As a personal trainer I became incredibly popular and could hand pick my clients. They'd pay anything I asked. But I came to realise the majority weren't concerned about becoming fitter for the health benefits but for the boost it gave their outward appearance and what that could translate to in terms of their careers.'

Jane set down a steaming mug on his bedside table. 'Tell me more and you get these yummy Cornish shortbread biscuits.'

Hal swiped the packet she dangled from her fingers, ripped it open and crammed one of the buttery cookies in his mouth.

'Hungry?'

'A certain insatiable lady forced me to skip lunch.'

'Complaining are we?'

'What do you think?' He reached for her T-shirt, strictly speaking his T-shirt, and swept his hand up under before she firmly tugged it back into place.

'I think you're avoiding talking.'

'Yeah, I know. Sorry.' Hal explained all about setting up Pumping Gold and building up their client list to include a raft of household names. 'I didn't have time for a private life … or I guess I chose not to make time. The women I dated understood that.' He half-smiled. 'Mostly.'

'What made you give it all up? Because we both know it wasn't to write a book.'

He took a few sips of lukewarm tea. 'Does the name Kristen Weeks mean anythin' to you?' Jane's gaze flickered away. 'Damn it. Who told you? I suppose one of the SAPs?'

'No, it wasn't them. Philip mentioned—'

'—I should've guessed.' Hal sagged. 'My damn cousin was right again.'

'What's Sam got to do with this?'

'She found out via the Muir family gossip line and challenged me last week.' He planted his hands on his knees. 'Sam told me I should come clean about it all before you heard a half-assed version from someone else. Trust good old Philip to beat me to it.'

'Don't do this, Hal. He was trying to wind me up.' She touched his cheek. 'Only you know the real truth and that's what I want. I waited for you to tell me because I knew you would.'

Her trust awed him. 'It's not pretty. Hollywood is brutal, particularly on women and Kristen was a little-known actress who couldn't accept that her limited shelf-life was coming to an end. She begged me to work her hard enough to compete with actresses twenty years younger.' He couldn't look at Jane. 'I've always been strict about my clients sharing the results of regular physical check-ups with me but … she lied. She'd been diagnosed with a heart condition and warned to avoid strenuous exercise. After a particularly gruelling session she collapsed and died right there in the gym in front of me.'

'Oh, Hal. I'm so sorry. That's awful but it wasn't your fault.'

'Wasn't it?' He sprang off the bed and paced around the room. 'I bought into the sick culture that drove her to think that was necessary. In fact, I made a fuckin' fortune from it.' Hal planted himself in front of Jane. 'Everyone tells me I shouldn't feel guilty but I'm still struggling to get my head around it. The paramedics had to drag me off Kristen because I wouldn't stop performing CPR on her. I was so damn desperate to make her breathe again.' He blinked away a stinging rush of tears. 'Do you know what got to me the most? My other clients all expressed their sympathy but not a single person questioned the ethics of my behaviour or their own for continuing on the same cycle. It's one of the reasons I fought my attraction to you. I didn't believe I deserved to be happy.'

'Oh, Hal. Everyone does.' He watched her nibble her lip. 'I used to worry how my family would cope if I got seriously involved with any man and even considered the possibility of a life apart from them.'

'And now?'

'I think they'd survive. In fact I'm sure they would

be absolutely fine. They've changed and I have too.' She gave him a searching look. 'I completely understand why you feel the need to make a clean break from the fitness business. I'm sure it will be far healthier for you physically and mentally. By the way, does Cadan know about all this?'

'Cadan? I don't know. I suppose Sam has told him. He hasn't said a word to me.'

'He went through the mill with his ex-wife and losing little Mikey. If anyone understands about guilt, it's Cadan. Will you at least think about sharing this with him, please?'

'I guess I could.' Hal wasn't convinced it would help but refused to spoil another moment of their precious time together. 'That's enough of my sob story.'

'It's not a sob story!'

'Yes it is.' He lifted her lush mouth to his for a lingering kiss. 'That's better. How about we test out that bath-tub you were drooling over earlier before an early dinner? We can make our spa bookings for the morning. Cadan strongly recommended the couple's massage.' Hal plastered on a wide grin, only half needing to fake it.

'I'll bet he did.'

'So?'

'Sounds wonderful.'

He loved Jane more than he'd ever thought possible for playing along.

'Goodness, I'm stuffed.' Jane pushed away the empty plate. If she'd left one crumb of the delicious chocolate and apricot torte it was only because she was too well-mannered to lick the plate. Luckily, they were still in the run-up to Christmas and the quiet, elegant restaurant wasn't too crowded. The Cornish-led menu with most of its ingredients sourced locally was everything they'd been promised and more. 'That was divine.'

'I wouldn't have guessed.'

'I'm not the only greedy one. Your mincemeat filo cracker didn't stand a chance either. Trust you to pick the closest thing to mince pies on the menu.'

They'd proved earlier that two people, even when one of those people was a rather muscular American, could fit into the generously sized bath-tub, although the floor suffered from their exuberance. After mopping it up they'd enjoyed a detour via the bed before getting dressed. Now she totally got what the fuss was all about, although Jane couldn't blame her ex-boyfriend. They'd both been barely eighteen and equally clueless. She preferred not to over-think about the other women Hal had slept with but decided to be grateful for the experience he'd gained. Nothing about their lovemaking had been awkward and that was mainly down to him.

He reached for her hand and a hint of thoughtfulness dimmed his smile, enough for someone who knew him well enough to notice. 'I didn't get far talkin' about my folks earlier. They're good people and didn't deserve the bad choices I made as a teenager or the way I've neglected them since.'

'Isn't neglected a bit strong?'

'Not really. Oh, I've phoned on the expected holidays and birthdays, but I discouraged them from visiting California by spinning the lie that I wouldn't have time to see them. Until I saw my folks on the way here, I hadn't been home for ages and never around the holidays.'

She didn't want to come across as critical, but her mother and Nick meant everything to her and Jane couldn't imagine not moving heaven and earth to be a part of their lives even if she had her own family one day.

'Don't worry. I don't expect you to understand because I don't myself.' Hal shrugged. 'At first I was ashamed for anyone to know the golden boy was reduced to scouring the grocery store at midnight for almost out of date food on sale. When things picked up, I guess I'd got into the habit of flying solo.'

'And now?'

'It's lonely.' She was shocked when she realised tears were glistening on his blond eyelashes. 'Bloody lonely. Everything's changed since I met you. You've turned my life 360 degrees and that's awesome, but I'm achin' to put things right with my family.'

'The New Year's a great place to start.' Jane cleared her throat. 'I'm planning to make a few changes too.'

'You're gonna start by winning this competition and becoming a best-selling author.'

'Oh Hal, be realistic. The chance of winning is miniscule but the best-selling part is less likely than me being the next British astronaut on the space station.'

'All right, Little Miss Practical. Tell me what've you got in mind.'

She hadn't shared this with anyone because something about going back to school at her age sounded faintly ridiculous. Haltingly she explained her plan to study part-time for her A-levels at the local college in St. Austell. 'I need those first and then—' Her cheeks heated '—I'd like to go on to do an English degree. But I've got to keep working while I do all that because living on fresh air wouldn't suit me.' Jane patted her stomach.

'That's awesome and I'm certain you can do it.' Hal's gaze bored into her. 'I've gotta believe that next year's gonna be a good year for both of us.'

For so long the thought of another January arriving meant more of the same, not necessarily bad but not exciting or challenging either. Apart from falling for this incredible man she'd finally arrived at the conclusion that the responsibility for her own happiness lay with her and no one else.

'We're on the same page again.'

'Talkin' about pages, when you gonna show me that book you've written?'

'Show you?' Jane panicked. 'I don't know. When I entered this competition it was the first time I'd ever shown my writing to anyone. I'll have to think about it.'

'Heck, if I'd asked you to strip naked and dance on the table, I don't think you could look more horrified.'

Of course his rumbling laughter caught the waiter's attention and the young man immediately came over to ask if they needed anything. She pressed the pink linen napkin over her mouth to stifle her laughter and stared down at the table.

'Yeah, we'd like a bottle of champagne for our room.'

'I'll have one brought up, sir.' He disappeared towards the bar and Jane's giggles erupted.

'You owe me a naked table dance for savin' you there, sweetheart.'

'In your dreams.'

He winked and tapped his forehead. 'It's lodged right there. Permanently.'

With as much dignity as she could muster Jane rose from the table, treated him to a sweet smile and exited the room. He'd discover his mistake in teasing her when they reached the bedroom.

# Chapter Sixteen

Someone must make a fortune selling the mildly irritating ethereal music all spas played as a background soundtrack. Hal relaxed as the young woman worked oil into his shoulders and he sneaked a peek from under the mask covering his eyes as Jane moaned with pleasure while her own masseuse worked a similar magic. After a swim in the heated infinity pool they'd enjoyed the sauna for a while before showering together. Stretched out on adjoining tables and covered with warm white towels, this was their final treatment.

'Please take your time before you sit up again and there are two glasses of water on the table. We'll leave you to get dressed and come out when you're ready.'

As the door closed Jane's soft laugh echoed around the room. 'Is someone going to put the bones back in my body?

'You liked that?' A ridiculous smile creased his face.

'No. I didn't like it … I absolutely adored it.'

'So, if I learned how to do that you'd be putty in my hands?'

'I am already.'

Hal eased up to sitting and swung his legs around to face her. 'I think I was the manipulated one last night.' She'd discovered her power over him when they returned from dinner and, in the best possible way, made him pay for his naked dancing comment. No wonder they slept through breakfast and made yet another meal out of tea and biscuits. 'Here you go.' He passed a glass over to her. After draining his own in one long swallow he stood up, dropped his towel and reached across to whisk hers off.

'Are you mad? They might come back in.'

'Just helpin' you out.' He laughed. 'Get dressed woman. We're goin' back to the bedroom.'

'But the weather's so pretty. I thought we might take a walk before lunch. The grounds look beautiful even though it's wintertime.' Jane's hand strayed temptingly downwards. 'Perhaps you'll convince me otherwise?'

'There's no "perhaps" about it.'

'Stop bragging.'

'I'm tellin' it like it is.' Hal pulled away and reached for his clothes. 'Come on, let's get out of here.'

They reached their room and made the most of the luxurious bed and massive bath for the last time.

'Does brunch sound tempting to you? The menu looked decent.' He glanced back over his shoulder while he combed his hair. She didn't take an eternity to get ready like most of the women he'd known and was already reading a book and waiting on him. His revelation about Kristen Weeks didn't seem to have changed Jane's feelings towards him, which he should have guessed by the way she treated her family and friends. Jane didn't give her affection and loyalty lightly but, when she did, they were unshakeable. When they returned, he'd make sure he had a quiet word with Philip Bunt. The man needed to know that hassling Jane crossed a line Hal wasn't prepared to ignore.

'Brunch would be wonderful, but why are you frowning?'

A small white lie wouldn't hurt. 'I can hardly believe it's Christmas Day next week and I haven't bought any presents yet.'

'Presents?'

'Yeah, the—'

'—things people buy to exchange on the twenty-fifth of December? I've heard of them,' She quipped. 'I haven't bought mine either. I'm way behind this year.'

'Anybody would think you'd been … tied up or somethin'.' Hal deservedly earned a sharp poke in the ribs.

'Mum's normally done a lot of baking by now, but it'll be shop-bought mince pies and Christmas cake this year. I'm only happy that she's so much more content now she has her job and Nick will cram in anything that resembles food so he certainly won't care.'

'Normal teenage boy.'

'He is and I'm grateful.' She untucked her legs and came over to join him. 'One kiss and then we're going downstairs to eat. I refuse to be forced to lie excessively when people ask whether we enjoyed the food here.'

'I'll give the biscuits ten out of ten.'

'And me?' Jane wound her fingers behind his neck.

'You're off the scale.' He squeezed her tight and made the most of his one rationed kiss.

They parked outside her house but neither rushed to get out of the car. Although they'd talked about a lot of things one still hung over them.

'I can't take advantage of Sam and Cadan's hospitality indefinitely.' Hal had guessed where her thoughts were going which shouldn't have surprised her. 'They won't want me under their feet once the baby arrives. That's what's made you sad isn't it?' Hal pushed a lock of hair away and kissed her cheek. 'Oh, and giving up that awesome bed and amazing bath-tub.'

'You know me well.' The weather had altered for the worse since this morning and the leaden sky, heavy with threatening rain, suited the downturn in her mood. Sitting here surrounded by Hal's warm, musky scent made everything worse.

'You and me. Doesn't make sense in a few short weeks, does it?'

'No, but a lot in life doesn't make sense.' Jane sighed. 'I'd better go in. I've seen the curtains twitch a couple of times and Mum will want the full rundown.'

'Being a good writer, I hope you'll edit it first?' Hal grinned.

'Yep, she'll definitely get the 12-A rated version.'

'I guess it's similar to our PG-13?'

'I suppose.' She played with the ends of her red wool scarf. 'At thirty-five it shouldn't be a problem if I go away with my ...' Jane suddenly realised what she was about to say and paused '... boyfriend?'

'Don't tiptoe around me. You're not goin' to frighten me off putting a label on me ... on us.'

'But you—'

'—shied away from it before? Yeah, but that was then and this is now. It's about you not any of the other —'

'—shush.'

'Is it all right if I come in to say hello?'

'I'd like that. If you're lucky there might be an uneaten mince pie or two lying around the kitchen.'

'You've talked me into it.'

'Doesn't take much where those nasty things are concerned. In case I haven't said it enough already, thank you for a wonderful time.'

'I'm the one should be thankin' you. Let's call it a draw.'

*They had to make this work. All this love couldn't fade back to nothingness*, she thought to herself.

'That's better. You're smiling again. I watched you argue it through in your head and knock that insane little wobble back to the kerb where it belongs.' He grasped hold of her face and weaved his fingers up through her hair so she'd nowhere to look but his penetrating blue eyes. 'I get them too, not gonna pretend I don't but one way or the other we'll sort this out … you believe me?'

'Yes. Yes I do.' Jane opened the car door. 'Come on, boyfriend.'

'I'm guessin' you finish college on Friday?' Hal asked, and Nick threw him a wary look.

'Yeah, until the week after New Year.'

'Got any plans? Apart from updating the church website of course.'

'Funny.' Nick swallowed another mince pie nearly whole.

The Christmas lights were on when they walked in and the radio in the background was playing festive music which made poor Jane wince. He had a personal weakness for any songs connected to the holiday because they stirred up ingrained memories from his childhood. Some of the tunes here were unfamiliar but enough were universal and brought a lump to his throat.

'Are you much of a runner? You've got the build for it.'

'Runner? Not really.' Nick shrugged. 'They made us do some in school and I guess it was okay.'

Gaz Menear's father had made a comment that stuck in his head about the village teenagers being bored because they didn't have enough to occupy them. At the time Hal thought it a convenient excuse on the part of a largely absent parent but had mulled it over ever since. Two weeks off school in the middle of winter with none of a small child's excitement surrounding the holidays was a recipe for trouble.

'I've been running each day to help keep the mince pies at bay.' He patted his stomach. 'You could join me.'

'Me?'

'Yeah, and any of your friends could come along too. The more the merrier.'

'But it's wintertime. The weather's lousy.'

Jane's eyes sparkled. He'd made a successful career out of motivating people disinclined to exercise and one uninterested teenage boy wouldn't faze him. 'Maybe Demelza would like to come too. She looked like she might be quite into fitness. Does she live around here?'

'In St. Petroc.' Before Val or Jane could ask who he was talking about Hal nailed home his advantage. 'Mutual interests are a good start. How about Saturday morning at nine?'

'Nothing else to do, I suppose.'

'Let me know if you rope anyone else in so we can decide where to meet.'

Nick rolled his eyes. 'Got an essay to write.' He sloped out of the room and both women turned to stare at Hal.

'Where did that mad idea come from and who's

Demelza?' Jane launched at him. 'Apart from one of the main characters in the *Poldark* books.'

Hal briefly explained about meeting the girl Nick had a crush on. 'Don't you dare tell him I spilled the beans or he'll kill me.'

'We won't and I don't think it's a mad idea at all,' Val chimed in. 'Anything that keeps him out of mischief must be good. Maybe he can rope in that other pair of reprobates?'

'Gaz and Sprout?' Hal could tell Jane's horror had zoomed off the scale. 'We're trying to get my brother away from their influence, not tangled up deeper.'

'Hey, if you don't have the early shift at work you could come with us,' he suggested.

'Me? Now you've really lost your mind.' Her gaze turned more piercing. 'When did you dream up this little scheme? You never said anything to me.'

He could hardly admit the germ of the idea snaked into his brain last night when he lay awake watching her sleep next to him, wondering what else he could do to convince her this wasn't a fleeting holiday romance. 'I was gonna ask what you thought, but it sort of popped out before I had the chance.' Hal didn't ask her to repeat what she was muttering under her breath but guessed it was on the lines of that being typical for him. 'I ought to be goin' now.'

'I'll see you out.'

'Bye Val, and thanks for tea.'

'Anytime, my 'andsome.'

At the door Jane's smile faded.

'You won't like me saying this but if this idea of yours extends past Nick you need to be careful. Make sure you get another adult along with you. Dr Menear will nail you to the wall if his precious son claims you've worked him too hard, and it's the sort of thing that boy would do for the hell of it.' The edge to her voice softened. 'You mean well. I totally get that, but I'd hate to see you in trouble through no fault of your own. You've been there already.'

Hal felt uncomfortable at the reference to Kristen but realised Jane was right.

'You could ask Tim Farnham,' she continued. 'He's run a lot of 10Ks and coastal path races. Last October we all sponsored him to do the Eden half-marathon.' Jane rested her hand against his cheek. 'It's a great idea and I love you for coming up with it.'

'Is it because you're a writer that you always come up with the right thing to say?'

'Don't be daft.'

'You're working tomorrow?'

'Yes, early shift. I'll be home by five at the latest but before you suggest anything, I'm going to the Kaolin Singers' Christmas concert in the church at seven o'clock. You're welcome to join me.'

'But you hate Christmas music?'

'I don't hate it per se. It's having my ears bleed from listening to it day in and day out for an inordinate number of days at work that drives me crazy. Anyway Pat, Lisa and Heather are all in the choir so that means—'

'—mandatory attendance by the more vocally challenged SAPs?'

'Who said we were...?' Her smile widened. 'Oh, very funny I'm sure. We'll find out who's the vocally challenged one in the singalong at the end.'

Hal could have mentioned his solos in the high school choir but a man needed to keep some surprises in his arsenal.

'Afterwards Fliss and Jory have invited everyone to the pub for mulled wine and—' Jane grimaced '—your favourites of course. Unfortunately it's the easy refreshment option for every Christmas function.'

'How about I pick you up around half six? I assume your mum is coming too?'

'Yes, I'm sorry, but it's one of her favourite things about Christmas and she'll probably drag my brother along'

'Never apologise.' Hal grasped her shoulders. 'One day you'll meet my lot and, trust me, your small family's got nothin' on the Muir clan.'

For a moment she was speechless.

'And yeah, that's a promise.'

'Good.'

Each time they inched one more step forward Hal held his breath waiting for panic to swamp him, but so far all it felt was damn good.

# Chapter Seventeen

'You sneaked out on me Sunday. I was hoping to finish our conversation.' Philip angled his body so she couldn't walk around him, trapping Jane between the freezer storage and the back door.

'If you check you'll find I clocked out on time.'

'You know that's not what I meant.'

She shivered under his scrutinising gaze.

'I'm guessing you had a good time with lover boy? I suppose he took you somewhere expensive and was paid back in kind.'

Did denigrating her really make him happy? 'What's wrong, Philip?' She kept her voice light. 'It hurts when you talk to me this way.'

'Didn't it sink in when I told you I love you?' He grabbed her arms, dug his fingers into her soft flesh and pinned her against the stainless steel freezer.

They were the only people left in the shop now, so it was no good expecting anyone to rescue her. 'Yes, it did. We've been good friends for a long time … at least I thought so and for me that's …'

'… enough?' Philip scowled. 'Well it's not for me.'

'I'm really sorry but you can't make someone … care.' Her avoidance of the L word made his face darken. The last thing she needed financially right now was to lose this job, but he was making it impossible for her to stay. She could report his behaviour to the manager but where would that leave her? The rest of the staff would claim, rightly, that they often spoke and laughed together. Jane would get the blame for leading on a decent, respectable man who was good at his job. Suddenly someone banged on the door.

'Jane, are you in there?'

The relief of hearing Hal's deep drawl made her knees buckle.

'I thought I'd surprise you with a lift home. Save you catchin' the bus.'

Philip froze and she took advantage of his momentary lack of concentration to wrench out of his hold.

'Jane, what's goin' on? I'm gonna break in if you don't—'

'—I'm fine.' She pushed the door open and fell into Hal's arms. 'Oh, I'm so glad to see you.'

'Well I'm glad to see you too, but—' He frowned back over her shoulder at Philip, white-faced and silent '—did he hurt you?'

'No, we'll talk about it later. Okay?'

'Are you sure?'

'Yes, let's go.'

Hal glared at Philip. 'Apart from anything that's strictly work you'd better stay away from her, mate. She's made it clear she's not interested so get the hint and back off. That goes for all other women too. If they say no they mean no.'

Philip turned bright red. 'I'd never ... this is personal ... Jane realises that.'

'Of course I do.' She turned to Hal. 'I'm perfectly capable of ... dealing with this myself, thank you very much.' Jane prickled. His macho attitude irked her, but she also resented the nagging sensation that she'd been daft enough to allow herself to get in this situation in the first place. 'I'll only be a minute. I need to get my bag and coat.'

'Jane, I'm sorry.'

For a few brief seconds Philip's shaky voice stirred her sympathy but this man who claimed to be her friend had frightened her, and she couldn't see any way of coming back from that. She unhooked her coat from the rack on the wall, hitched her bag on her shoulder and swung back around to Hal. 'Let's go.' Jane wasn't sure she'd ever be able to return.

Hal kept the conversation innocuous on the drive home. It took him about five minutes to drag the first laugh from her with his story about a confrontation with a herd of sheep being moved from one field to the other while he was running along one of the narrow lanes near Gweal Day. 'The farmer didn't look too pleased, so I hung back and let them do their thing.' Taking advantage of her softening mood he kept going. 'My dear cousin is now fully in what Cadan informs me is nesting mode. He's read every pregnancy book on the market so I'll defer to the expert because he assures me it's common. It seems to involve cleaning and scrubbing everything in sight, cooking more food for the freezer than they'll eat in a lifetime and organising all the cupboards so no one but Sam can find anything.'

'Scary.'

'Yeah, I was lucky to escape without having bleach chucked over me.'

'I assume they're going to the concert tonight?'

'Oh yeah, Sam's not goin' to leave a mince pie unscathed in Little Penhaven if she can help it.' He stopped outside

Jane's house. 'You wanna talk about what happened with Philip and why I pissed you off? If I offended you, I sure didn't mean to.'

'I know.' She exhaled a weary sigh. 'I overreacted but he'd rattled me.'

Hal's grip on the steering wheel tightened as she explained what happened. He wasn't a violent man but a powerful urge to plough his fist into Philip Bunt's smug face swept through him. 'You know it wasn't your fault, right?'

'In theory but—'

'—there's no "but" involved.'

'Just like there wasn't with you and Kristen Weeks?' A heavy silence filled the car as he pulled to a stop outside Jane's house. 'Now I'm the one who's sorry,' she said.

'No, you're right. I'm a hypocrite. I guess we both need to forgive ourselves.'

'You mean that?'

'Yeah. Yeah, I do.' The burden he'd carried far too long began to loosen. 'Deal?' He pulled her close for a kiss. 'That's better. I got cheated earlier.' Making one thing absolutely clear to her was essential. 'When I threatened Philip it wasn't because I see you as a weak woman who can't speak for herself ... but I love you so much and part of that is being on your side, standing with you, supporting you.' He watched as Jane's soft eyes glazed with tears. 'If it came across any other way, I'm sorry.'

'We've a lot to learn.'

'There's time and I know that bothers you, but we'll be okay.' Hal stroked his hand over her silky hair and a drift of her familiar tropical shampoo teased his senses.

'I think you're probably right.'

'One day soon I'll make you sure and that's a promise.' *Making those was becoming a good sort of habit*, he thought to himself. 'What are we doin' now? You want me to come back later to pick y'all up?'

'No, you're not going anywhere except inside the house with me. We always cook plenty of food to cover Nick's voracious appetite so I'm sure tea can stretch to feed one more. I don't suppose you need to go back to Gweal Day and change into any Christmassy clothes?'

Hal grinned and unzipped his jacket to show off a new bright red jumper. The front boasted a gaudy green felt Christmas tree topped with a gold star and covered in dangling baubles.

'Wow, it's, um, festive.'

'Sure is. I picked this little beauty up in Truro today. It's a neat little town and I wrapped up my Christmas shopping.' He laughed. 'Literally.'

'Good for you.' Jane's smile wobbled. 'Maybe I'll do mine tomorrow.'

'I thought you had to work?'

'I don't see how I can go back in.'

Hal was conflicted. The idea of her going anywhere near Freshlands and Philip Bunt nauseated him, but she needed the money. She'd rightly be offended if he offered to help her out financially because the same pride kept him away from his family while he struggled to keep his head above water in California. But pride only worked in small doses and the key was in knowing when to concede and accept help.

'Maybe I can pick up a few hours in the pub. Fliss and

Jory will be swamped over the holidays.' She frowned. 'Please don't mention the trouble with Philip when we go in. It'll only worry Mum.'

'How's that goin' to work when you don't go in to Freshlands as scheduled?'

Jane shrugged. 'She knows I hate working there. I'll say I've had enough and plan to look for something else in the New Year.'

*She won't believe you for a minute. You're transparent as glass but I'll back you anyway.* He kept the thought to himself.

'Thanks, that's all I ask.'

The way they saw right through each other baffled and awed him.

'Will this do?' Jane posed at the top of the stairs. 'I'm not attempting to compete with your fashion extravaganza.' The combination of much colder weather and the meagre heating system in the old granite church meant she could get away with wearing the only red top she owned; a soft cashmere turtleneck she'd bought in the January sales.

'Perfect.' Hal's eyes brightened.

Compliments embarrassed her and his obvious admiration mixed with her brother's loud snigger and her mum's flagrant wink made her face heat up to match the jumper. 'Are you all ready?'

'Just waitin' for you, sweetheart.'

It would have been a pleasant walk in the crisp night air but her mum wouldn't be able to manage it, so they piled in to Hal's car.

'If we added in a touch of snow this would look like one of those Christmas card scenes,' Hal said, thoughtfully.

'All those mince pies must be affecting your brain.' Jane had grown to love Little Penhaven over the years but in a clear-eyed, realistic sense. Even a layer of fresh white snow wouldn't wave a magic wand over the plain, unobtrusive village and turn it into one of the picture postcard tourist spots Cornwall was famous for. The people and sense of community were what made it special.

'The car park will be full. Do you mind dropping us outside the church and Nick can help you find somewhere to park? White River Lane should be a good spot.'

'Sure.'

Her mum shivered when they got out and tightened her scarf around her neck. 'Brr, do you think that awful Beast from the East thing is going to get us again?'

The Cornish didn't handle bad weather well. A few centimetres of snow and the county ground to a halt. The freak snowstorm that blanketed the area for a few days the previous March was ingrained in people's memories and panic re-emerged every time the temperature dropped.

'No, Mum. But it is Christmas next week so having to wear our winter coats and wrap up a bit isn't exactly unusual.' Jane linked her arm through Val's. 'Come on, let's go in and find a seat.' A loud hum of conversation filled the crowded church as people vied to be heard over the organist already playing Christmas carols.

'We've saved you four seats.' Cadan waved at them from the front and they made their way down to him.

'Careful, Mum.' Jane dodged the fresh greenery wrapped around the stone pillar and avoided the strings of fairy lights draped overhead to slide into an empty seat. 'How's it going, Sam? I hear you've been busy.'

'I suppose this one—' Sam shot a fierce glare at her husband '—and my pest of a cousin have been complaining? The pair of them don't have a clue. This poor kid will come home to a filthy house and nothing to wear if I don't watch out.'

Before she got pregnant Sam was the least domesticated of the SAPs. She loved ripping walls down and plonking in bathrooms but everyday dusting didn't interest her and neither did cooking.

'You look positively Madonna-ish tonight.' The dark blue dress sprinkled with silver stars and moons fell in soft drapes over her friend's baby bump and she'd swept her long black hair back in an elegant French pleat to enhance the effect. Cadan rested his hand on Sam's stomach and gazed in adoration at his wife.

'Any room for two little ones?' Hal's husky drawl startled her, and Jane's heart almost stopped beating as their eyes locked.

*I want this. I assumed I didn't, but I want it and I want it with you.*

She put the rush of emotions down to them being stirred by her friends' encompassing love, the sentimentality of the season and the organ playing her favourite carol, "In the Bleak Midwinter", softly in the background. Really it was far more.

'Haven't people here seen a Christmas jumper before? Everyone stared at me.' Hal squeezed in next to her.

'They probably haven't seen one worn by someone …
like you.' *Tall. Blond. Muscular. And with a face like
Adonis if he'd had a wicked streak*, she thought.

Tim Farnham clapped his hands and, by the time he'd
finished introducing the choir, the wave of chatter quieted
down. Hal laced his fingers through hers and dropped a
soft kiss on her cheek.

'Cadan's a lucky man,' he whispered. That was his way
of letting her know he understood.

Jane let her head rest against his shoulder until the first
half of the concert finished.

'Were we very awful?' Lisa appeared, followed close
behind by Pat. The red bows the twins had added to their
normal black and white choir outfits matched their shiny,
anxious faces.

'You were great.' If asked she actually couldn't have
said what they'd sung because her mind was too wrapped
up in other things.

'We prefer the old-fashioned carols we sing in the
second half. If you're in a pensive mood, you'll find the
frozen gardeners' song will get to you but if you want a bit
of fun it's hard to beat "Stuff Your Guts".'

'Sounds intriguing. Where's Heather?'

'Gone to see Mole of course. They're like two strips of
Velcro these days.' Lisa rolled her eyes and pointed across
the church.

'Time we went back.' Pat tugged her sister's sleeve.
'We'll see you in the pub later.'

'That's a thing I've never heard said in church before.'
Hal laughed. 'Works for me though.'

'Right everyone.' Tim got the congregation's attention.

'We're going to enjoy four more songs from the choir then it's time for all of us to stretch our vocal cords.'

'Don't worry, honey. I'll cover for you,' Hal teased.

'You? I'm sure.' She nudged her mum. 'Make sure you listen out for Alfie Boe here.'

'Who is he? I've never heard that name before.'

'A popular British singer.' Hal's smug expression didn't falter as she nestled into him.

# Chapter Eighteen

Hal considered holding back but couldn't help himself when the organist struck up the opening chords of "Joy to the World". By the time it finished Jane wasn't the only one staring at him slack-jawed.

'Why didn't you warn me?'

'Warn you? Was it that terrible?'

'You know what I mean,' she hissed.

'You've got a decent voice too. You don't caterwaul.'

'Oh thanks, Mr Pavarotti.'

Hal felt embarrassed. 'You're exaggerating.'

'Not much. I expect to hear more about your vocal abilities later.'

'Yeah, no problem.' He picked up the hymn sheet and treated her to a long, slow wink. 'Off we go.'

After they wrapped up with a few more carols a grey-haired woman with a no-nonsense glimmer in her eyes bustled up to the front of the church.

'Good evening, everyone. For those of you who don't know me I'm Cynthia Bullen, head of the parish church council.'

He picked up on a few quiet groans and rolling eyes.

'Our retiring collection is for the children's refugee fund. Most of us will enjoy an abundant Christmas next week and so the least we can do is give generously to those who are less fortunate. We're all invited to go into the Queen's Head now where the landlord is providing mulled wine and mince pies for everyone free of charge.' The glint in her eyes deepened. 'However, the collection box will be there too.'

'So that's the infamous Mrs Bullen?'

'Oh yes. She sorted out Sam and Cadan and is a great one for doling out advice even if people haven't asked for it.' Jane snorted. 'In fact, particularly then. You'd be wise to avoid her. I've got to be brave and speak to her because I never thanked her for helping Nick.'

'She's not all bad then?'

'I never said she was.' Her face brightened. 'She's a more outspoken version of Miss Marple.'

'I bet you've used her for one of your characters?'

'Henrietta Morley might have hints of good old Cynthia, not enough she'll recognise herself but—'

'—*you* know?'

'Oh yes, *I* know.'

'Are we all ready?' Cadan draped his arm around Sam's shoulder. 'If this lady doesn't get a mince pie in the next five minutes my life won't be worth living.'

Making their way through the crowd wasn't easy but Jory had reserved their favourite large table in the back corner again.

'Here you go, Cade. Quality time with your nephew.' Jory plonked the fussy toddler in his brother's lap. 'Ten minutes, mate, twenty tops. Fliss is up to her eyeballs and we're knee deep at the bar. Her parents went to the concert, so they'll put Kit to bed when they've had some refreshments.'

'You're managing?' Cadan jiggled the little boy and a smile wreathed his round pink face, lighting up his huge blue eyes and making his white-blond curls bounce around his head.

'Yeah, can't complain. I'll catch up with you later. If I don't get back to work now Fliss and John will have my guts for garters. Carol singing makes for thirsty customers.'

'Talking about work, when are you back in next, Jane? Tomorrow?' Val asked.

A tinge of colour flushed her cheeks. 'No. I won't be going in tomorrow or any other time because I quit. I'm not working there any longer.'

'What on earth do you mean?'

Last time Hal interfered it didn't go down well, but he took a chance. 'She's got reasons, Val. Good ones, including simply wanting a change.' That put the ball firmly in Jane's court.

'He's right, Mum. I'll tell you more about it later.' Her quick hand squeeze under the table encouraged Hal to hope he hadn't said anything out of line. A mischievous smile turned up the corners of her mouth as she fixed her gaze on him. 'And you can buy me a packet of cheese and onion crisps.'

'They go well with mulled wine?'

'Better than those lead weights you're consuming.'

'Eating onions isn't a smart idea if you're going to be kissin' anyone later,' he whispered.

'Then you'd better man up and eat some too.'

No competitive athlete turned down a challenge and when Hal returned from the bar to dump a large mound of crisp packets in the middle of the table he ripped one open, flashed a grin at Jane and popped one of the pungent crisps in his mouth.

'Your American is an interesting man.'

144

Cynthia's observation made Jane's face burn.

'First Cadan and now you. I don't know what the world's coming to. Half the population of Little Penhaven will be American if this goes on.'

Any form of denial would get her in deeper trouble.

'I have to say that everyone I speak to praises him up. Apparently he and Tim Farnham are starting some ludicrous scheme to wear out the village delinquents by turning them into competitive runners.'

'That's an exaggeration.'

'Maybe, my dear.'

'I never had the chance to thank you for—'

'—there's absolutely no need.' Cynthia held up her hand. 'The appalling Colonel and that awful Virginia have the Christian compassion of a pile of rocks. I've known dear Nick since he was knee-high to a grasshopper and he's on his way to turning into a fine young man. He had a little wobble. We all do. But he doesn't need to pay for it in blood and the other boys don't either, although the Menear and Hooper lads do need reining in before they get in serious trouble.'

Jane's eyes stung. 'Whether you like it or not you're not going to escape without hearing how grateful we are. Mum ... hasn't had things easy but things are looking up now.'

'I rather think her little job was one of my better ideas.'

'Yours?'

'I was talking to Jenny a few weeks ago ... don't think we were gossiping, it was simply interest in a friend's welfare. Everyone needs a purpose in life and to feel valued. Poor Valerie had lost that.' Her countenance altered. 'I'm not a vindictive woman at heart but Ralph Davy should pay for the way he treated her.'

'She doesn't want that.' Jane trotted out the whole explanation. 'I've just managed to track him down and he's back living in St. Agnes again.' Last night when she'd finished doing some research on untraceable poisons for the next chapter of *A Cornish Casualty* she had the sudden urge to Google her stepfather. Almost too easily she had found his address. 'I could contact him through a solicitor.'

'Face to face. That's the best way.'

*Exactly what her character Henrietta Morley would say*, Jane thought with a smile.

'I suggest taking your handsome young man along to put Mr Davy in his place. With his size and all those muscles, he is rather imposing … until he smiles.'

Cynthia Bullen had a soft spot for Hal? Now she'd heard everything.

'Oh dear, every woman in here will fall in love with him now.' Cynthia nodded across the room. 'You have a serious rival for his affections.'

Hal stood near their table rocking from one foot to the other with an idiotic smile on his face and Jory's little boy, slack-mouthed and fast asleep, plastered against his shoulder. Kit hadn't stayed quiet with Cadan for long and Fliss's parents hadn't appeared, so they'd taken it in turns trying to pacify the fractious child. Jane did a great job with him until she spotted Mrs Bullen and tried to pass him back to his uncle. The change startled him awake and he'd wailed loud enough to be heard over all the noise. That's when Hal stepped in.

'There's nothing like the sight of a grown man caring for a child to melt women's hearts.'

Admitting she was a puddle of mush herself would be a waste of breath judging by Cynthia's knowing smile. 'I'd better go,' she said.

'I won't bother telling you to be careful because it's plainly too late for that.'

'It's never too late.' All of her common sense hadn't flown out of the window. Life had taught her caution.

The only reminder left when Fliss's mother came to retrieve her grandson was the damp patch of drool on his jumper. Despite being an only child, by circumstance not choice on his parents' part, there'd been no shortage of Muir cousins around when he was growing up. Hal had become the go-to boy they all wanted to play with until he decided it was beneath his stroppy teenage self to bother with the little kids. The lifestyle he'd drifted into didn't encourage family life and that hadn't bothered him until a couple of years ago. When he turned thirty-five it was as if the endless string of marriage and birth announcements from his extended family only emphasised the emptiness he felt rattling around his huge, empty house.

'Do you miss your shoulder ornament?' Jane popped up by his side. 'Of course you've got plenty of others on your tacky jumper, but they aren't as cute as Kit.'

'True.'

She gave him a pensive smile. 'Did you know Cynthia Bullen is a paid-up member of your fan club?'

'Uh, no. Do I even have one?'

'According to her most of the women in Little Penhaven

have joined. Married. Single. Old. Young. Apparently it doesn't matter.'

'Does to me.' Hal snuck his arms around her waist and yanked her close. 'There's only one woman interests me and I'm holdin' onto her.' He stroked her silky hair. 'Shouldn't we be gettin' on back to your place? Nick's got school tomorrow and isn't your mum working?'

'Aren't you a thoughtful man?' Jane's eyes shone. 'It's got absolutely nothing to do with sneaking some time on our own of course.'

'Of course not. My mama brought me up to think of others first.' A pang of guilt engulfed him. He'd tossed away so many of the values his parents drummed into him or at least buried them so deep that people who never saw past his surface didn't realise they were there.

'I honestly could do with leaving anyway, because I'll have to brave the crowds of late Christmas shoppers tomorrow.'

He considered offering to join her but took a guess she'd rather go alone, plus there were things he needed to sort out, not least of which was calling his folks. They might not say he owed them an apology but he knew he did. Right now he'd snatch a little more time with Jane before facing the music.

Later in the evening, as the clock struck eleven, he struggled to quell his nerves and picked up the phone.

'Hal?' His mother's voice rose. 'This is a surprise. We didn't expect to hear from you until Christmas.'

'Am I interrupting your dinner?' It was six o'clock in Knoxville, their usual meal time, but he was pretty sure they wouldn't care.

'That doesn't matter.' She briefly went quiet. 'Is something wrong?'

Hal's throat tightened. 'Yes and no. Put the phone on speaker please. Dad needs to hear this too.' No way could he say everything twice.

'Okay.' The dragged out reluctance in her voice made it clear he'd worried her. 'Your dad is here listening.'

He plunged into an apology for his teenage behaviour, the thoughtless way he ran off to California and his subsequent lack of contact. 'At first I couldn't see any other way to sort myself out. And later on it seemed ... too late.'

'It's never too late, son,' his father chimed in.

'I realise that now. Do you think the rest of the family will forgive me? I really need them to.' Hal's voice broke with emotion.

'Of course they will. You show me one of them who hasn't made a mistake along the line and I'll show you a liar,' his father said in his no-nonsense manner.

'The other big thing I need to get off my chest is that I lied to you both when I left to come over here. I'm not writing a book. I never was.' His mother's laughter tinkled down the phone and he could picture her shaking her head. 'You didn't believe me anyway, did you?'

'Of course we didn't but we reckoned you had your reasons for spinnin' a yarn. To our way of thinking you needed a break after all that trouble in California and to find a different path in life. It sounds as though you've done that, so it's all good.'

His mother's astute summing up blew him away but who knew him better? 'You're right. I've been talkin' to a few people here and I've come to accept my role in Kristen

Weeks' death. I'm not proud of it and I'll always carry a measure of guilt but I guess most of us do that for one thing or another.'

'We sure do.' His father joined in. 'When are you goin' to bring this cute little girl we've been hearing about from Mary Ann over to see us?'

Hal chuckled. 'I should've guessed that piece of news wouldn't surprise y'all. I haven't asked Jane yet, but I'm thinkin' early in the New Year if I can talk her around.'

'Sounds good. Now off you go. This is costin' you a fortune.' His mother's urging made Hal smile. 'Our fried chicken is gettin' cold.'

'Criminal.'

'It sure is, son,' his father chimed back in. 'Now do what your mom says and hurry home soon.'

'I will.' For the first time in years he'd sleep with a clear conscience.

# Chapter Nineteen

With only five shopping days left until Christmas, Truro was a mad house. Jane caught the bus because the idea of fighting for a parking space was too disheartening, but it only gave her a minor reprieve from the chaos. The pavements were jam-packed and, judging by the amount of jostling and sharp comments flying around, the unavoidable piped Christmas music in every shop and street decorations weren't completely successful in stirring up a goodwill-to-all-men effect. Jane pulled up her collar, tugged on her red wool gloves and prepared to battle the bitter wind. Hal had got his wish for cold weather, although thankfully there wasn't any snow in the forecast.

The SAPs' tradition was to meet on Christmas Eve to swap presents. With a five pound limit and all of them having different tastes, it was a challenge to find something unique. She took a short cut in through the Pannier Market and stopped to admire a display of Christmas goods outside the flower shop. Jane spotted some miniature Christmas trees decorated with simple gold balls and stars on top. She thought she must be reading the price wrong but checked the ticket again and smiled. The perfect height to sit on a table-top, they'd be ideal for those who didn't have a lot of space and shouldn't clash with anyone's colour scheme.

'Could you put five of these back for me ... no, make that six?' One could decorate Hal's bedroom at Gweal Day. 'I'll pay you now and pick them up on my way back to the bus.' With that organised she headed towards the back of the market.

'Oh, Jane!' Mandy Johnson, one of the Freshlands cashiers, turned bright red when they almost bumped into each other. 'What on earth happened to you? Why did you leave us in the lurch in the middle of crazy season?'

Her boss wasn't happy when she quit without giving a week's notice, but she'd decided missing out on a pay packet was better than facing Philip again. 'I'm sorry but I really needed a change.'

'That's the excuse he gave too.'

'Who?'

'Mr Bunt resigned the same day as you. Didn't you know?' Mandy's gaze darkened. 'Most people think you planned it together. They have you marked down as a couple.'

'And you?'

'I would've agreed at one point but that day I walked in on the pair of you, he was all over you like a rash and I didn't get the impression you welcomed it.'

'You're right. They're wrong.' Jane exhaled a heavy sigh.

'You should've reported him if he got a bit ... you know.'

'It would be my word against his and everyone knew we were good friends. It's not a huge step from that to something more. If I thought he was a threat to you or any other woman I would've pursued it but it was ... personal. I'm sure you realise that.'

'Of course I do. We both know if it was otherwise that those kind of rumours always get around. I've never heard anything negative said about Mr Bunt.'

'You're right, nothing stays a secret at Freshlands for long,' Jane mused.

'I'll still miss you though.'

'I'll miss you all too, but it was time for me to move on. In an odd sort of way, it's probably all for the best.' She hadn't realised the truth of that until this moment. 'I must be going. I've lots more shopping to do. Happy Christmas.'

Three hours later she made it back to Little Penhaven and clambered off the bus, completely exhausted from standing all the way holding bags in both hands and with more stuffed on the floor between her feet.

'Care for a ride home?' Hal appeared from nowhere and whisked the shopping out of her numb hands.

'Are you an angel in disguise?'

'Nah, just a friendly devil.' He gestured towards his car. 'Come on, before you freeze to death.'

'This is your fault. You wished for wintery weather.'

'Yeah well Cadan's fretting about it big time. He's convinced Sam will go into labour early and they'll be trapped behind a ten-foot snow drift at Gweal Day.' Hal grinned. 'I told him I'd watched a YouTube video on deliverin' babies but that didn't seem to help matters.'

'Can't imagine why. Be careful of those.' She retrieved the bags containing the miniature trees before he could toss them in to join the heap on the back seat.

'Dare I ask …?'

'No.'

'Fair enough. Hop in.'

Jane chattered all the way home about meeting Mandy and the nightmare of pre-Christmas shopping in Truro. When they stopped outside her house it suddenly clicked that he hadn't said much apart from the occasional nod and mumble of agreement. Very unlike him. Hal normally didn't hold back on expressing his views.

'I've promised my folks I'll be back early in the New Year.' He'd been easing around to telling her ever since he picked her up. 'I called them when I got back to Gweal Day last night and apologised for the way I've treated them. It was a start but I need to visit. Talk face to face. You know I have to. I can't—' he seized her hands '—move on with you until I put things right with my family. I've been an ass.'

'You won't get any disagreement from me.' Jane's humour lifted his spirits.

'Would you consider comin' with me?'

'Me?'

Hal exaggerated looking around the car. 'There's no one else here so I guess I'm talkin' to you. They've already heard about you from Sam's mother and if we're goin' to … I mean … I need y'all to meet up and … Oh Lord I'm makin' a right mess of this.'

A slow, beautiful smile lit up her face. 'I'm happy that it's a million miles from a smooth, practised speech. That would worry me.' She touched his face. 'This is real.'

'It sure is.' Leaning in for a kiss he hesitated. 'I brushed my teeth multiple times, but I can still taste those nasty chips from last night.'

'Nasty? You clearly don't have a sophisticated palate.' Jane giggled. 'Of course you've proved that by loving mince pies.'

'Hopefully it won't prove an irreconcilable difference between us.'

'I think we can work around it. You'll have to promise not to force mince pies down me and I'll only eat cheese and onion crisps when we're not going to be … doing this.'

Her hot, lingering kiss made Hal's head spin.

'I wish we were on our own somewhere too,' she whispered.

'You never answered my question about coming to Knoxville with me and, before you worry about the cost, I invited you so I'll pick up the tab.' He laid his fingers against her lips. 'Please don't argue. I want to do this … for us. It's a way of tackling one obstacle that's all.'

'You're devious.'

'Good devious or bad devious?'

'On the whole I'd have to say good.'

He hadn't realised he was holding his breath until he wasn't any more. 'Fantastic.'

'Thank goodness I got a passport for Kate's hen party in Turkey or we'd be out of luck. I think it only takes a matter of days to get an electronic visa for the States so that shouldn't be a problem.'

'So, you'll come?' Hal's amazement must have showed because she gave a broad smile and nodded. 'You want to tell your mom now?'

'I don't see why not.'

'Come on then. I'll get your shopping.'

'I'll carry the bags that need a little more … care.' She hopped out and picked out what she wanted on the back seat.

He didn't have a clue how she'd managed to haul all this lot around Truro and on the bus but kept his mouth shut and did as she'd asked. Hal was learning.

*

'Hello, Mum. We're back.' Jane's high spirits bubbled over. The living room's tired wallpaper and worn paint looked more on the lines of shabby chic tonight under the twinkling Christmas lights.

'When were you going to tell us you'd found him?' Nick leapt up from the sofa and waved a scrap of paper in her face. Her own unmistakeable large loopy writing where she had copied her stepfather's current address down stared back at her.

'What were you doing poking around in my bedroom?'

'That's my fault.' Her mother interrupted. 'He needed a pen and none of the ones down here worked so I sent him to find one on your desk.'

'Where I bloody found it doesn't matter.' Nick looked livid.

'You're right and I'm sorry.'

'Do I get an apology too?' Val chided her. 'You should've come to me first when you found Ralph.'

'Oh Mum, you're right too of course.' Jane sunk onto the nearest chair. 'I thought if I could get him to agree to a divorce it would be a nice surprise.' That had come out wrong. 'Not nice exactly but …'

'You meant well. I know that.' Her mother patted her shoulder. 'You've been taking care of us all too long, and it's hard to break the habit.'

'I'm going to see him in the morning,' Nick announced. 'I've checked on the buses and when I get to Truro I can pick up one from there to St. Agnes.' The stubbornness running through his voice warned her she'd have an uphill battle to dissuade him.

'I'm not sure that's a smart idea. I was planning to ask Hal—'

'—Hal?' Nick glared. 'No offence, but this is none of his business.'

Poor Hal looked totally confused. She wished she'd got around to telling him about finding her stepfather and asked his advice on how to proceed. The easy excuse was that there hadn't been a good moment, but she should have made one.

'Is there any chance of putting these down somewhere before my hands fall off?' He held up her shopping bags.

'You do that my 'andsome and I'll stick the kettle on,' her mother offered.

Jane stood the other bags with the trees in carefully on the table and hurried into the kitchen. 'I'm really sorry, Mum.'

'I know you are, love. We'll talk while we have a cup of tea and decide the best thing to do. I bought a box of iced Christmas cake fingers. Jenny ordered too many and they aren't selling well.'

She wasn't a huge fan either but would force one down to keep the peace. Soon they were all settled in the living room and Jane tried to answer her family's questions. 'It seems Ralph was working up in Devon for a while but has drifted back down this way.' Her mother couldn't hide her dismay when she revealed Ralph was living in St. Agnes again with another woman and had fathered two more children.

'You lot can talk around it all you want but I'm sticking to my plan.' Nick stormed off.

'I'd better go after him,' Jane said, beginning to move towards the stairs.

'Give him space,' Hal urged. 'He needs to process it all. I'm happy to drive y'all in the morning if you want?'

Jane nodded, biting back tears.

'Why don't you give your mom a bit of good news instead?'

Before she could speak her mum engulfed her in a tight hug.

'You sneaky thing. It's quick but you're old enough to know your minds.' Val stepped back and grabbed Jane's left hand. 'Show me the ring.' Her enthusiasm dialled back a notch. 'I don't suppose you've had time to find—'

'—we're not engaged, Mum. Don't be silly!' Out of the corner of her eye she caught Hal's smile fade.

'Our good news is that Jane's coming with me to visit my family early in the New Year,' he explained.

'That'll be lovely. Sounds expensive though.'

'It's …' Jane wasn't quite sure how to put it.

'… a Christmas present.' He came to her rescue. Again. 'Although it's as much for me as her so I'm guessin' she'll expect something else on Christmas Day.'

The conversation slipped into plans for the holidays, a much safer subject than why she had been so shocked at her mother's assumption while Hal had simply looked disappointed.

# Chapter Twenty

Hal could hear Cadan's electric sander from outside the shed and knocked a couple of times before opening the door.

'Have you come to finish off Jane's present?' Cadan turned off the noisy machine.

'Uh, not really. Although I guess I should.'

'Too early for a beer?'

He wasn't meeting Jane until two o'clock so had several hours free yet. 'Nope, about perfect I reckon.'

Cadan pulled a couple of cans out of the fridge and offered one to Hal. 'Get that down you. Is something up?'

'Not sure.' He popped open the beer and took his time finishing it. No wonder his voluble cousin and this quiet, thoughtful man made such a great couple. He guessed Cadan's quiet patience was cultivated during the years when he'd been ostracised from the village with no end in sight. When he explained his reaction to Jane's scathing dismissal of her mother's assumption that they'd got engaged it sounded ridiculous.

'You wanted her to be all giggly and coy.' Cadan gave a wry smile. 'But that's not our Jane. She's learned not to expect much and would hate you to think she assumed anything, especially this soon. Don't forget she's lived with the fallout from her mother's rushed marriage to that Davy fellow and she's probably afraid of following suit. You'd already made the perfect move inviting her over to Tennessee then her mum essentially spoiled it.'

'You reckon?' His jangled emotions settled back down. 'There's a lot to be sure of before we … get to that point.' Hal cracked a smile. 'But I reckon on gettin' there sooner rather than later.'

'Good.' His friend picked up a sheet of sandpaper from the workbench. 'While you're here do something useful apart from drinking my beer. That needs a final rub down.' He pointed to the chair leg he'd been sanding.

They worked away quietly until lunchtime.

'Time to check on the bleach queen.' Cadan chuckled. 'Last night I caught her on her hands and knees scrubbing the bathroom floor with a toothbrush. How she bloody well got down there in the first place is beyond me. I had to haul her up and it nearly did my back in.'

'Not long to go now.'

'Four weeks if she's on time.' Deep furrows etched in his brow. 'At yesterday's check-up the midwife didn't seem to think it would be that long. She spouted a lot of baffling statistics about measurements and where the baby's head is. I'm keeping up with the weather forecast and plan to whisk her off to Treliske if one flake of snow falls.'

Hal struggled not to smile.

'But she totally gets why this is freaking me out while I tolerate her disinfecting everything in sight.' Cadan's face softened. 'We're trying to reassure each other everything will be fine but neither of us will really relax until this little munchkin arrives safely.'

'I'm takin' a guess most new parents are the same.'

'You're right. My carefree brother became so uptight, and don't get me started on Fliss. She veered between hormonal floods of tears to a frantic whirlwind of cooking and often sent Jory out in the middle of the night searching for ingredients. There were enough lasagnes and cottage pies in the freezer to supply the pub kitchen for months when Kit was born.' He motioned for Hal to go out and locked the shed.

'Life eh?' Hal smiled. 'Thanks for the bolsterin' up mate.'

'Any time.'

Jane pulled Hal out through the kitchen and into the back garden, desperate to apologise before they left for St. Agnes. 'Mum has decided to stay here because she can't face seeing Ralph again but Nick is coming with us. He's getting ready.'

*You sneaky thing. It's quick but you're old enough to know your minds.* At the time her mum's words had whirled madly around on a hamster wheel in her head. Val always said that she and Jane's father were wildly happy right up until he died, but that she made a mess of everything when she fell for Ralph Davy's shallow charms. After Hal left yesterday she thought things through more clearly and concluded once and for all that Hal wasn't Ralph. He was ten times the man her stepfather had been. Make that a thousand times.

'I had a chat with Cadan this morning.' He slid her a sideways glance. 'Want to know what about?'

'I'm sure you'll tell me.'

'He's a sharp guy.'

A couple of minutes later she couldn't decide whether to be pleased the two men got on so well or mortified that they'd discussed her unflattering reaction over their non-engagement.

'He was right, wasn't he?'

Jane nodded.

'Good.'

'I'm sorry if I—'

'—no need. I'm glad we've cleared it up.'

The fact he meant every word proved his love for her far more than any extravagant bouquet of flowers or expensive box of chocolates. 'I do love you.'

'Yeah, I know.' Hal flashed a wicked grin. 'Gweal Day's gonna be unoccupied for a few hours tonight because Sam and Cadan are off to a party at the Bullens' house. Would you like to come and see the Christmas decorations in my room?'

'You've got more than the tree I bought you?'

'Wait and see.' He winked. 'Let's round up Nick and get on the road.'

Five minutes later they were off, but between Hal's need to concentrate on navigating the unfamiliar roads, the damp dreary weather and the prospect of what lay ahead of them, they were a silent trio.

'Davy's house should be along here.' Hal signalled. 'Seaview Road sure isn't living up to its name today.' A thick blanket of fog surrounded them, making it impossible to see more than a couple of metres in front of the car. 'There's number fifteen.'

The terrace of plain granite houses all bore signs of Christmas but number fifteen in the middle boasted the most with an inflatable snowman and plastic reindeer on the scrubby front lawn and flashing Christmas lights looped over the prickly evergreen bushes.

Nobody rushed to get out of the car. When they eventually

made a move Jane clutched Hal's hand. Nick dragged along behind as they made their way to the front door and she wondered if he was having second thoughts about coming.

'If you're carol singers, forget it.' A tired-looking, washed-out blonde woman jiggling a fussy baby peered out at them.

'We're looking for Ralph Davy.'

'Who is it, Annie?'

A tall, thin man appeared at the top of the stairs and bile rose in Jane's throat.

'I dunno. They want you. I've got to put this one down for a nap.'

'Here I am what do you—' Ralph turned pale ' —Jane? Jane Solomon. Goodness you're all grown up.' Despite his thinning hair and tired deep-set eyes, his eerie resemblance to Nick unnerved her.

'It's been seventeen years.'

He gave Hal a wary glance. 'Who's he?'

'Hal Muir, my boyfriend.'

'What're you here for ... oh my God.' Ralph glanced behind her at Nick and every remaining drop of colour left his face.

'Could we come inside for a few minutes?'

'I suppose.' He could barely drag his eyes off her brother. 'This way.'

They followed him into a small untidy kitchen.

'My mother wants a divorce,' Jane blurted out.

'Uh right. No problem. We should've done it before. I never got around to bothering because I wasn't in a rush to get married again.' Ralph shrugged.

'Would you like to say hello to your son?' She tugged

Nick's arm and when he stepped forward the two stared at each other without speaking.

'Son?' Annie reappeared without the baby. 'This boy is your son? You never told me you've got another child.' She peered at Nick. 'He's the bloody spitting image of you!'

Ralph ignored her. 'Did Val call you Nicholas?' His voice thickened with emotion. 'That's what we agreed we'd call the baby—'

'—before you did a runner?' Her brother's mouth curled up with scorn. 'Yeah, I'm Nick, and I doubt you could care less but my mum still suffers from a bad knee because of what you did to her.'

'I never meant … it was an accident.'

Jane scoffed. 'Even if it was that doesn't alter the fact your eight months pregnant wife fell down the stairs and you left without helping her. She and Nick could've died for all you cared.'

'You never did?' Annie stared at Ralph in horror.

'I panicked. I've been expecting the police to knock on my door all these years.'

'Mum never wanted that.' Jane explained her mother's wishes. 'All she wants is to be rid of you legally.'

'Tell Val I'll sign anything she wants and that I'm sorry. Really sorry.' Ralph hugged Annie. 'It's no excuse but I was young and stupid back then. I hope I'm a different man now. We've got the two kiddies, little Ralphie's nearly six months and Flora's almost two. She's with Annie's mum down the road today.' He fixed his weary gaze on Nick. 'I know it doesn't make up for not being a father to you, but I'm trying my best to be a good dad to them.'

For a fleeting moment she felt sorry for him. Ripping

him away from his new family and wrecking two innocent children's lives would be heartless. Jane understood her mother's choice to let things be far better now. 'You ready to go, Nick?' His brooding silence worried her.

'Yeah.'

'I get that you don't want anything to do with me,' Ralph muttered, 'but if you do decide to come back here again any time—'

'—don't hold your breath.' Nick grunted. 'I've heard enough.' He pushed past them all and slammed the front door on his way out.

'You still don't have a clue about the impact you had on us all, do you?' Jane couldn't leave without saying her piece too. 'You damaged my mum in so many more ways than the lasting physical effects and she's only now regaining her confidence. I suppose you might've thought about her and Nick occasionally but I'm pretty sure I never crossed your mind. I was simply the unwanted teenage girl you got lumbered with.' She glared at the man who'd haunted her far too long. 'For years I've been wary of men because I assumed they'd treat me the way you did my mum. It's taken the kindness of friends, watching good relationships work and—,' she smiled over at Hal '—the love of this wonderful man to help me through that.'

'Anything I say is going to sound pathetic, but I'm glad you're okay now. Nick seems—'

'—angry? Frustrated?' Hal interrupted. 'Yeah, he's all of those things but he's also a kind, smart young man who has two amazing role models in Jane and her mother. They've sacrificed a whole lot to bring him up right and you should be damn grateful to them.'

'I am.' Against her will Ralph's defeated expression touched her.

Outside Hal wrapped his arms around her and a sweep of weariness engulfed her whole body. She spotted Nick with his shoulders hunched, hands shoved deep in his pockets and staring morosely at the house.

'Time to head home, sweetheart.'

'Could you ever think of it that way?' Jane tripped over her words. 'I don't mean that Tennessee wouldn't always be ... you know what I mean, at least I hope you do.' She grimaced. 'I'm doing the babbling thing again. Sorry. But I just don't know if I can ...'

'You're gettin' ahead of yourself.' His piercing blue eyes bored into her. 'Every couple makes compromises and even those aren't set in stone ... unless one of them is a sculptor.'

'Very funny.'

'I thought it was a pretty darn good too.' He used his remote to open the car. 'Jump in, Nick. Let's get going.' He gave Jane a quick squeeze. 'I think it's time to enjoy one of the Christmas presents I've bought you.'

'Dare I ask?'

'Nope, but I promise it doesn't involve mince pies.'

*God, but she loved this man.*

The cold starry night reminded Hal of winter in the Smoky Mountains and he sucked in fortifying breaths of the crisp air. He'd never really settled into the southern Californian climate and missed the more distinct change of seasons he'd grown up with. He'd followed Nick outside to the back garden because Jane asked him to see if he could be of any help.

'What did *you* make of him? My so-called father.'

He didn't reply right away, unsure how to answer. Val had listened to everything Jane had to say, asked a few brief questions then thanked them and claimed she needed an early night. Nick hadn't opened his mouth. 'Not much at first.'

'But?'

'He recognises he screwed up big time with you and your mom. Don't you go thinkin' a minute that I'm makin' excuses for Ralph, but he was too young and immature to be married with a teenage stepdaughter and a baby on the way. He couldn't cope.' Hal shrugged. 'He can't see a clear way to putting that right now, so all he can do is try to make a better job of it this time around.'

'I suppose.'

'We all struggle sometimes. I haven't shared the worst of mine with you.' He quietly explained about Kristen Weeks' tragic death, his devastation at not being able to save her and his growing revulsion surrounding the industry that he'd made his fortune out of. 'It's all about choices, Nick.'

'So, what are you going to do now?'

'I'm a bit like you there because I'm not sure.' Hal grinned. 'I'm still a fitness nut and can't see that changin', but I'm mulling over a few ideas of how to use my skills better. Ask me again after tomorrow morning. I might change my mind after I've tried to turn you and your mates onto regular exercise but I'm thinkin' that something on those lines appeals to me.'

'It'll be bloody freezing.'

'Builds moral fibre. The vicar's rounded up half a dozen

or so from what he said. You'll get a chance to impress Demelza.'

'She's coming?' Nick's face flushed.

'Yeah, apparently her mum's in the church choir even though they live over in St. Petroc and Tim was spreading the word about our initiative so she got talked into it too.' Hal winked. 'My guess is she didn't take much convincin'. You'd better get a good night's sleep.'

'You're weird sometimes but Jane has a thing for you so I'm bloody sure we're stuck with you.'

He took the roundabout compliment the way it'd been intended. Teenage boys didn't exactly dish those out in spades. 'We'd better get back inside before she starts to fret, plus I'm takin' her out for a while and it's getting late.'

'Spare me the gruesome details.' Nick's smile broadened. 'Cheers for everything today.'

'No problem.' Now he'd enjoy getting Jane back in the festive spirit.

# Chapter Twenty-One

'Wow, as we say in the South you look like you've been rode hard and put up wet!' Sam's loud guffaw made Jenny Parson stare and Jane dragged her friend outside the shop before she became the focus of village gossip. 'The first time I said that to Cadan, I thought he'd die laughing when I explained what it meant.'

She didn't need a British/American dictionary because her friend's blatant wink did the job perfectly.

'I hoped I'd run into you.' Sam fished around in the battered leather satchel she used in place of a handbag. 'I hope this is yours, otherwise your man is playin' away.'

Jane swiped away the scrap of red lace dangling from her friend's fingers and shoved it deep in her coat pocket. 'Couldn't you be a bit more discreet for once?'

'And spoil the fun? No way. I don't get much of it these days in between peeing every ten minutes and needing a crane to get in and out of bed.' Sam grinned. 'Before you ask, your boyfriend's lousy at tidying up. I popped in to leave a couple of clean towels on his bed and voila!'

'I'm sorry ... we shouldn't have ...'

'Why not? Wasn't it any good?'

'Yes, but—'

'—excellent. We're happy to further the cause of love.'

'We? Cadan knows?' Could this mortification get any worse?

'Yeah, we don't have any secrets.' Sam smirked. 'Unless you count whatever he's been working on for my Christmas present and that's allowed.'

Jane allowed a smile to creep out. 'At least we didn't pollute Cadan's precious woodwork shed.'

'Hey, you do what you gotta do.'

'Are you two planning a quiet weekend?'

'Is that a subtle way of asking if I've finished copying those demonic women on the TV where they're cleaning filthy houses?' Sam chuckled. 'Yeah, I think it's out of my system but now that's worryin' poor Cadan because he thinks it's a sign I'm ready to go into labour.'

'Do you fancy a coffee in the pub? Hal's meeting me there after he's finished dragging the so-called Little Penhaven running club out to your place and back. He said that was a long enough distance for him to size them up.'

'Sure. Why not?'

They wandered along Fore Street, enjoying a good-natured chat about their friends along the way.

'Hello, ladies.' Jory stopped in the middle of refilling salt shakers. 'What can I get you?'

'Two Americanos with hot milk. A couple of Fliss's divine mince pies too for me and the little one.' Sam cradled her mountainous stomach. 'Where's Kit today?'

'Meeting Father Christmas at Dairyland. He'll probably scream at being plonked in the lap of a huge man in a red suit with a bushy white beard. I predict frazzled grandparents and an exhausted little boy by the time they return.' His smile deepened. 'Bloody good job I'm working the late shift because he'll be bouncing off the walls tonight. Go sit yourselves down and I'll bring the coffees over.'

The door opened and a cold blast of wind sliced through the warmth from the blazing fire in the corner as a noisy crowd of people jostled their way in.

'Hi, gorgeous.' Hal lifted Jane off her feet in a hot, sweaty hug. 'I'm treating all the ones who've survived to a drink.' After a hard kiss he set her back on her feet. 'Jory, get them a pint of iced water each before they have any sodas. One for me too please.'

'I'm eighteen—'

'—I don't give a monkey's ass.' He cut off Gaz Menear's whine. 'I'm almost thirty-seven and you won't see me drinkin' alcohol after exercising. It's not smart. You need to rehydrate properly.'

'Over here.' Sam had staked a claim on the window table.

'You dropped me in it with your cousin.' Jane lowered her voice. 'Remember the new red lace item I couldn't find last night? She found it.'

'Shit.'

By the time she gave him a quick run-down they were both pink-faced and laughing.

'Mind if we join you?' Tim Farnham shepherded the teenagers over to sit down.

'Did it go well?' Jane spotted Nick lurking as far away from them as he could manage. She wouldn't be tactless and ask for an introduction to the smiling, red-haired girl hanging onto his arm. Not yet.

'Yeah, we weeded out a couple of nuisances pretty quickly but I reckon the rest might stick with it.'

'You enjoyed it.' They'd spoken last night, in between doing other more adventurous things, and he'd asked her opinion about the idea he'd floated to Nick. Jane could already tell by the conversations around her that the young people had warmed to him, respecting his experience but appreciating his down-to-earth manner. 'I feel the same satisfaction when a character develops seemingly by magic but really it's the result of hard work.' She glanced at Sam's untouched plate. 'Aren't the mince pies any good today?'

'I'm sure they are. It's me. I don't seem to fancy them.'

'You sure you're all right?'

'I'm tired. I think I'll head on home.'

'Did you walk?'

'Yep, I thought it would do me good.' Sam's smiled appeared forced. 'Not sure it was a smart choice.'

'I'll run you back,' Hal offered. 'I've got to shower and change anyway before Jane will want anythin' more to do with me the rest of the day. I'll get the car and pick you up outside.'

'There's no need.'

'Yeah, there is or the Muir family mafia will come down on me like a ton of bricks for not lookin' after you.'

Under the smile Jane knew he meant every word.


By the sidelong glances they'd received Hal got the impression that the hospital maternity unit wasn't thrilled with them filling up the waiting room. The SAPs were determined they'd be there to welcome the group's first baby if they had to stay all night. By the time they reached Gweal Day before lunch he'd taken an educated guess that Sam's pallor, the wave of nausea making her open the car window despite the frigid temperatures and the way she constantly rubbed her lower back were hints that the newest member of the Day family would make an appearance sooner rather than later.

When his pale-faced cousin tentatively announced that she was in early labour and her contractions were getting closer together Cadan immediately returned to his usual steady, pragmatic self while Sam took his place as the nervous, jittery wreck of the family. He'd calmed his wife, collected their bags and the checklist he'd perfected over the last nine months.

'If you wouldn't mind letting the girls know we're headed for Treliske we'll meet you down there.'

'Me too?'

'You might as well. They're coming, it's all planned.' Cadan's borderline resigned tone made him smile. 'If you stay with Jane long term you get them all too. They're a package deal.'

Looking around him Hal decided they resembled the old women gathered around the guillotine in the French revolution without being either old or waiting to see someone's head chopped off. Kate was furiously knitting something yellow and fluffy, he assumed in an effort to beat Baby Day's arrival. Heather was studying a bridal magazine and occasionally showed a page to her friends. That would kick off a serious discussion about the merits of strapless sleek as opposed to extravagant princess gowns amongst other supposedly important topics. Pat and Lisa had their head stuck in books, obviously the same title because they'd occasionally argue about a certain chapter.

And Jane? She was scribbling furiously in a journal. He knew she'd plotted out and started writing her next book already but that her brain never stopped whirring and he suspected she'd been inspired with another fresh idea. Maybe it would feature a group of friends who, one by one, start to get murdered and her detective, Henrietta, would have to find the killer before they all die?

'Anyone want a sausage roll?' Heather offered a plastic box around.

Talk about coming prepared. Everyone had been assigned a particular food or drink to bring and he reckoned they had enough spread over the table to survive Armageddon.

'Thanks.' He popped one in his mouth and caught Jane's amusement. 'I'm a growin' lad.' She set down her notes and snuggled into him with a loud yawn. 'Tired?' Now almost midnight they'd been here for nearly twelve hours already. The last nurse they dared to ask how things were progressing told them in no uncertain terms that first babies are notoriously slow to arrive and to be grateful they weren't on Sam's end of the process.

'If I snore or drool poke me awake.'

'What if I'm doin' the same?'

She rolled her eyes. 'Useless man.'

'Charming I'm—'

The door banged back against the wall and Cadan stood there, grinning like a mad man with tears brimming in his bleary eyes.

'We've got a daughter. Can you believe it?' He waved his phone around. 'Kerensa Ann Day. Kerensa is Cornish for beloved one. She's eight pounds seven ounces and twenty-two inches long. She's the most bloody beautiful thing I've ever seen apart from her amazing mother. Sam swore like a trooper, refused any drugs and the staff here definitely won't forget her.'

The women rushed around him and oohed and aahed over the pictures but Hal hung back, feeling a little out of place.

'Sam wants to see you.' Cadan beckoned him over.

'Me?'

'Yes.' He grabbed Hal's shoulder. 'Her parents would've been here if Kerensa was on time and you're family so she wants you to see her first instead. Sorry, girls.'

'No problem,' Jane spoke up. 'We only came to be here for her. For you both. Give Sam our love and we'll see her and little Kerensa tomorrow. You're both exhausted.'

Hal didn't want her to leave. 'If you don't mind hangin' on, we'll ride home together. I won't stay long.' He gripped her hand. 'Please.'

A few minutes later when they placed the tiny, red-faced sleeping baby in his arms he couldn't meet Cadan's gaze. What strength did it take to survive losing his son but still experience incredible joy in the birth of his beautiful baby daughter?

'We've spoken to Mom and Dad briefly, but would you mind callin' them too?' Sam's tired face and lank hair were a clue to the hours of exhausting labour she'd endured but her grey eyes were shot through with silver and gleamed with love every time she glanced at her husband and new baby.

'Be happy to. Shall I take a few more pictures?' Once that was done, he left them alone and found Jane waiting outside the delivery room.

'Awesome, isn't it? I've never forgotten seeing Nick when he was a few minutes old.'

'Yeah, incredible. Ready to go home?' Hal managed a weary smile. 'And yeah I said that on purpose. Come to Gweal Day with me. I've got to call Sam's folks for a few minutes then I'm ... all yours.'

'Good, because that's exactly what I want you to be.'

He'd never heard anything better.

# Chapter Twenty-Two

Jane startled awake and couldn't work out why there were twinkling stars inside her bedroom. Only it wasn't her bedroom. The red and white Regency striped wallpaper, antique oak furniture and large brass bed proved that. So did the gorgeous naked man wrapped around her.

'Cadan's not comin' home tonight. He's crashing at the hospital.' He lifted her hair out of the way and sent feathered kisses shivering along her neck. 'You've proved yourself a huge fan of my Christmas decorations.'

She'd been astonished to discover he'd strung white fairy lights around his bedroom, bought a disparate collection of Father Christmas characters at the Truro market and draped fake greenery interspersed with red velvet bows around the marble fireplace.

'The Muirs don't do Christmas quietly. It's kind of a family thing. I'd have been laughed at in California where everything had to be fancy and colour coordinated, but now I don't care.'

'They're certainly a novel seduction tool.'

'Are they workin'?' He gave a wicked laugh when she pushed back into his searching hand. 'I'll go with a yeah on that one.'

'We ought to get some more sleep. We've got a busy day planned.' The SAPs were visiting Sam in the morning while Hal's Harriers, the joke name given to the running group by Sprout Hooper that she suspected would stick, were off on their second run. Then they were going to the church nativity play followed by Cornish carol singing at the Queen's Head and what Fliss was labelling a Cornish food extravaganza. Everyone else was calling it Pasty Night.

'I hope you're joking.' Hal rubbed against her, making it perfectly clear he wasn't the least bit tired, until she groaned. 'Yeah. Jokin'.' He flipped her over and proceeded to remind her how much and why she loved him, not that Jane honestly needed reminding.

Through a sleepy fog she heard a phone buzzing, decided it wasn't hers and poked Hal's arm. 'Your phone's making noises.'

'Right.' He tightened his arm around her waist and burrowed his face into her messed up hair.

'You ought to check. It might be Cadan.'

'What time is it?'

'Around seven, I think.'

He groaned and scrabbled on the table for his mobile. 'Shit.'

'Oh God, there's nothing wrong is there?'

'Don't panic. Everything's good. So good they'll be home in a couple of hours. Seems y'all don't keep them in hospital long.'

'It varies but Sam's disgustingly healthy and Kerensa's obviously fine, so I suppose it's reasonable.'

'Doesn't sound it to me but I'm a childless guy so what do I know?' Hal shook his head. 'Sending parents home so quickly with a little scrap like that would bloody terrify the life out of me.'

'Do you want kids?' *You don't have an atom of common sense. Way to frighten off a man in four simple words*, she scolded herself.

'Hey crawl down off the ceiling. There's no need to panic. If we don't ask each other important stuff, we won't know the answers.'

'And?'

'I don't randomly want kids with just anyone.'

Jane's heart leapt into her mouth. She'd taken it for granted they were in agreement, not that he'd specifically said so but ...

'You're jumpin' to the wrong conclusion.' Hal plastered her to his bare chest, making it hard to concentrate on anything. 'I'd relish nothin' better than having a whole bunch of kids with the woman I love and who loves me back.'

'A whole bunch?'

'Yeah. You weren't thinkin' the average one or two, were you?' By the gleam in his eyes Jane decided he was joking. 'Hey, if we're lucky enough to have any at all that would be awesome.'

'We?'

Hal cocked a quizzical smile her way. 'You weren't thinkin' of having them with anyone else, were you?'

Until she met him Jane was too focused on holding things together with her mum and Nick to allow dreams of marriage and a family of her own to intrude, except in the middle of sleepless nights when the thoughts wouldn't be quiet. 'No. You know there's no one else.'

'It's all good then.' He flung back the covers. 'I'd love to linger here with you all day, but I've got to tidy up around here some before I meet my running kids at nine.'

'Should I let the girls know? Did Cadan say?'

'Yep, he wants you to do your bush telegraph bit. Oh,

and Sam's folks are arriving tomorrow. There weren't many tickets available for flights landing on Christmas Eve but they paid over the odds for first class and managed to snag a couple. There's no way they were gonna wait until their scheduled travel date now.' Hal's colour deepened. 'I'm sure meeting you will be top of their list after they've seen the baby. My folks will have instructed them to interrogate us both and send back a full report.'

'Wonderful.' Jane squealed when he scooped her off the bed.

'Doesn't bother me.' He carried her across the room and flung open the window, laughing as a blast of cold air hit them both. 'I love Jane Solomon,' Hal yelled, his words flying away in the breeze.

'You're mad.'

'Yeah, but you love it.'

The words and his kiss warmed her all the way through.

'Should we clear out of their way?' Hal's question earned a raised eyebrow from Cadan.

The Gweal Day living room was jam-packed. Sam had issued a three-line whip bringing forward the SAPs' traditional Christmas Eve get-together a day to combine it with a meet-the-baby session. The piles of presents and abandoned wrapping paper had to be seen to be believed and he got a secret kick when Jane scored a big hit with her miniature trees.

'No way. We're on hospitality duty. Whatever they want it's our job to procure it.'

'Sam looks damn good to me. I expected her to crawl into bed when you got back from the hospital.'

'Me too.' Cadan chuckled. 'I could crash for about twelve hours straight if I had the chance.'

They both knew he wasn't complaining. The word besotted didn't begin to cover it.

'I suspect the post-baby hormones will plummet soon and she'll realise she's knackered.'

'We need more champagne—' Sam held up an empty bottle '—and you need to run down to Jenny's shop.'

'Why?'

'Because I'm dying for a Crunchie.' She gazed down at Kerensa. 'This little one messed me up, but now she's here I can't wait to sink my teeth into one again.'

Cadan winked at Hal and bent down behind the Christmas tree. 'See if these hit the spot.' He held out a badly wrapped parcel.

'Is this what I—'

'—open it instead of jabbering.'

'Here you go, Jane. It's your turn to hold her.' Sam passed Kerensa over and ripped open the box. 'Oh God, I love you so much, Cadan Day.' She dumped out a mound of chocolate bars on her lap and ripped one open, sinking her teeth in with an exaggerated moan.

Hal made his way behind the group and leaned in over Jane's shoulder. They locked eyes as he stroked the baby's soft pink cheek.

'Whatever your Crunchie equivalent is I'll get it for you. Anytime. Anywhere.'

'I'll do the same for you.'

'Track down some pecan Goo-Goo clusters in this Cornish wilderness and I'm yours forever.'

'Is that all it takes?' Jane whispered. 'You are easy.'

'I am where you're concerned.'

'Stop mooning over each other you two.' Heather prodded Hal's arm. 'This lot say Mole and I are glued at the hip but you're worse.'

The good-natured ribbing set off the others and soon he gave up and retreated to the safety of the kitchen.

'Sorry about that, mate.' Cadan stirred a heavy brown teapot. 'Ordeal by SAPs is a mandatory requirement if you're getting serious about one of them.'

'Reckon I'll pass the test?'

'You've got a pretty damn good chance. We're on your side if that helps.'

'Sure does. Anything I can do?'

'Help to wind the party down. My lady's fading but too stubborn to say so.'

'I'm on it.' Hal didn't have a problem with whisking Jane off somewhere on their own. That worked for the time it took to whisper his request until she reminded him they were due to pick up her mother for the nativity play and stay for the pub's pasty supper. It wasn't simply the girls' group he'd be taking on with Jane but Little Penhaven as a whole. He didn't mind in the slightest. Boy, how his Hollywood cronies would laugh. He didn't care about that either.

# Chapter Twenty-Three

'Do I look all right, Mum?' Jane screwed up her face in the mirror, trying to decide if she'd put on too much lipstick and if her new red wool tunic and black trousers fitted okay.

'Anyone would think you were meeting the Queen and Prince Philip.' Val frowned. 'I'm more worried what Mr and Mrs Muir will think of this place.'

'Don't be.' When Hal suggested bringing Sam's parents over on Christmas Eve for a casual lunch at their house it sounded a great idea. That was until her mum started to fret about what Mary Ann and Preston would think of their modest home and Jane worried herself silly about Hal's throwaway remark a couple of days ago.

*I'm sure meeting you will be top of their list after they've seen the baby. My folks will have instructed them to interrogate us both and send back a full report.*

'Everything's looking lovely and you know how down to earth Sam is so I can't imagine her parents being any different.' If she'd met the Muirs when they had visited Cornwall before she suspected her nerves wouldn't be as bad, but she'd missed them on both occasions.

'But pasties? Don't you think we should've made something a bit fancier?'

'No. Hal insisted that would be perfect. It's lucky Jenny didn't need you in today.'

'Heather's off work until after New Year now so she's coming in to help her mum out.'

'We'll be upstairs.' Nick wandered in through the back

door with Demelza right behind. 'Let us know when they're here.' The girl seemed to spend half her time at the house these days. They ran together each morning with Hal's Harriers and both worked in the pub when Jory needed extra help. Demelza had her heart set on becoming a doctor and hopefully the young woman's determination to do well in her exams and secure a place at a good university would be a positive influence on Nick.

Jane put some foil over the pasties so they wouldn't get too brown and was startled when the doorbell rang. 'I'll answer it, Mum.' She took a couple of steadying breaths and plastered on a smile. 'Hello, you must be—'

'—well aren't you the sweetest little thing.'

Engulfed in a perfumed hug, Jane wasn't sure how to respond. Nobody had called her that since she was a child and Mary Ann Muir was hardly a giant herself. Suddenly she was held out at arms' length and scrutinised by a pair of sharp, blue eyes.

'I'd say our Hal was right. He told us this morning that you were pretty as a picture, but I thought that was a lovesick man talkin'.'

'Stop embarrassing the poor woman.' Preston Muir almost crushed her hand with a vigorous handshake. Sam had clearly inherited her father's height and big-boned frame. 'It's mighty kind of y'all to invite us over. Is this your mama?'

Jane collected herself and introduced Val, then Nick and Demelza who'd appeared without having to be hassled.

'Wow, I can't believe I've met me a real live Demelza.' Mary Ann beamed. 'And a red-head like that cute Eleanor Tomlinson, although in the books she's dark-haired.'

'Oh Lord, don't get started.' Preston rolled his eyes. 'I'm afraid she's a *Poldark* nut.'

Everyone had heard about the mountain of *Poldark* memorabilia Sam's long-suffering father had lugged back to Tennessee after their first visit, including an appallingly heavy model of Wheal Grace.

'It's all right, Mrs Muir.' Demelza smiled. 'I love it too. My mum was a huge fan of the first series when it was on the telly back in the Dark Ages and that's why I got my name.'

'Do I smell pasties?' Hal sniffed the air and slipped his arm around Jane's waist, brushing a quick kiss on her cheek. 'You smell pretty good too.'

'Flatterer.'

'Jane, why don't you get everyone a drink while we all sit down?' Her mum asked. 'I want to hear all about little Kerensa.'

'Oh, you will.' Preston smiled at his wife. 'This one can't stop talkin' about her.'

'And you're not equally obsessed? She's only two days old and got you wrapped around her little finger already. The midwife is due to come by to see Sam and the baby, so this was good timing.'

'I'll help you.' Hal steered Jane towards the kitchen.

'But I haven't asked what they want?'

'We'll do that in a minute.' He toed the door shut and plastered her against the wall. The long, sensuous kiss he drew them into would have made her moan if she was trying not to draw attention to the fact they were snogging like teenagers within hearing of their families. 'Okay. Better we stop there.' Desire roughened his deep, smooth voice. 'Give Mary Ann a glass of sherry. Sam's convinced her that's what all Brits drink at Christmas and worked her way through half a bottle of Cadan's last night. Mixed with jet-lag, I'm surprised my aunt's still standin'. Preston's a beer man like me.'

'I'll take the pasties out to cool down. You can be barman.'

'Yes, ma'am. How about you?'

'I better fall in with your aunt's theory if I want to get on her right side.'

Hal stopped her with his hand. 'Hey, of course I want them to like you but it's not going to change my loving you if for some bizarre reason they don't. Please don't drink that nasty gloppy stuff for my sake.'

'Ah, we've finally found a Christmas treat you don't like.'

'Need a hand?' Nick stuck his head in around the door. 'I told them you were probably "busy" and no one seemed surprised.'

Jane gave a careless shrug. Hal was absolutely right. Their families were important but not enough to sway them one way or the other when it came to deciding their future together.

He dropped Val off in the village to have tea with Jenny, ran his aunt and uncle back to Gweal Day and took Nick and Demelza back to her house. Finally, he got Jane to himself. 'Lunch went down great. They're officially addicted to pasties now and with the amount of sherry your mom put in that trifle it's no wonder Mary Ann was giggling like a schoolgirl. In case you're wondering my dad and Preston are similar, in looks and temperament, but my mom and Mary Ann couldn't be more different,' Hal explained. 'Mom's far more reserved, a bit of an academic. She teaches English literature at the high school in their gifted programme. I'm sure you two will hit it off.'

'I'm looking forward to meeting them both.'

'Really?'

'Yes, why wouldn't I be?'

'You've been very quiet since everyone left. I thought you might be frettin' about meeting them.'

'I'm sorry. It's nothing to do with you, us, your family or Christmas, I promise.'

'You're nervous about the writing competition.' Hitting the proverbial nail on the head brought back her smile. 'There's nothing you can do about it. I'm sure it's all decided by now.'

'That's supposed to make me feel better?'

Hal shrugged. 'Worryin' about things you've got the ability to change is one thing, but this is out of your hands. Let's enjoy Christmas and I'm pretty damn sure the New Year's goin' to be a good one either way.' He ran his hands over her soft curves.

'Any idea how to pass the time until church starts at eleven tonight?' Jane gave a dramatic sigh. 'Something to help distract me?'

'Distractin' is my specialty, sweetheart.' Hal pushed her down on the sofa. 'Let's celebrate early.'

Much later he stirred awake and started to stretch before remembering Jane's narrow single bed didn't allow for that luxury. They'd moved upstairs after reaching their limits on the sofa. The bed wasn't a huge improvement but he could be inventive when necessary. A banging noise infiltrated his brain.

'Hey, gorgeous. I think someone's at the door. You want me to go see?'

'They'll leave if we don't answer.' Her husky laugh rumbled through him.

'Jane, I need to talk to you.' A man's voice yelled from outside.

'Damn, that sounds like Philip. I suppose I'd better—'

'—what's he doing here? No offence, but I'm comin' with you.'

'We might need to get dressed first.'

Tidiness hadn't been a priority earlier and it took a few minutes to track down their clothes and become vaguely respectable. Hal's hair wouldn't lie in place properly no matter how vigorously he combed it. 'That'll have to do.'

'Me too.' She gave a resigned look in the mirror. 'Come on, let's see what he has to say for himself.'

Nothing Hal wanted to hear that was for sure.

'This wasn't necessary.' Jane could hardly see Philip over the massive bouquet of red roses he'd thrust into her hands as soon as she invited him in.

'It's only a gesture and doesn't make up for my appalling behaviour.' He shoved a hand up through his hair. 'I can't think what got into me.'

If she wasn't careful Hal would spell out the answer in no uncertain terms. Very plainly he hadn't got the hint when she made it clear she didn't see him as anything more than a good friend.

'I couldn't believe it when they said you resigned too.'

Philip frowned. 'I never meant for you to lose your job. Why don't you ask for it back?'

'Because I don't want it back. I've got a few plans in mind, but that will be after I return from visiting Hal's family in America early in the New Year.'

'I hoped my mum wasn't right.' Disdain sneaked into his voice. 'She said there's no way you'd be bothered with me when you had a tame, rich Yank on a string.'

She could defend herself, but did she honestly care about the mean-spirited Eileen Bunt's opinion one way or the other?

'Time you left, pal,' Hal growled.

'It's none of your business.'

'That's where you're wrong.' She put her hand in Hal's. 'Go now and take these with you.' Jane shoved the flowers back at him. 'I'm sure your mother will appreciate them.'

He opened his mouth to speak then slammed it shut again. Hopefully it'd finally sunk in that there was nothing he could say that she wanted to hear. It was ridiculous to pretend they could ever be friends again. After Philip stalked out, she closed the door behind him and exhaled a deep sigh.

'No one else thinks I'm your tame, rich Yank on a string.'

Hal's quiet assertion stunned her. How did he understand her so well? 'And if they *are* idiotic enough to then they're the same as Philip's pathetic mother and not worth bothering with.' When his arms wrapped around her Jane's worries retreated. 'We both know that strictly speaking I'm not a Yank.' Hal smiled against her cheek. 'Yeah, I am well-off but anyone who really knows you isn't goin' to believe that matters for one second ... in fact they'd realise it was a definite mark against me where you're concerned.'

He was totally right. Again. 'Tame?'

'Oh, you've tamed me all right, but in the best way.' Hal flexed his impressive biceps. 'Doesn't emasculate me one bit.'

'I can vouch for that.'

'Hey, are there any Christmas movies on the TV?'

'Probably. Why?'

'We always used to watch—'

'—*It's a Wonderful Life*?' Jane grimaced. 'I should've guessed.'

'Christmas Eve tradition.' He made a grab for the remote control. 'It has to be on because I'm pretty sure there's an international law that you must be able to find it showing anywhere in the world at any time over the holidays.' Soon Hal grinned. 'There we go, it's just about to start.'

'Goody.'

'If you behave yourself and don't mock too much we'll watch *Bad Santa* after. I bet you've got the DVD?'

Jane flushed. The Billy Bob Thornton black comedy was a modern classic in her mind.

'If you're really in a sentimental mood I reckon you might stretch to watching *Elf*?' He grinned and settled on the sofa. 'Do you have popcorn?'

'No, but I could warm up some sausage rolls and mince pies?'

'Yeah, that'll be perfect.'

Jane snuggled into him and decided to watch with an open mind. She'd hopefully be watching the soppy film every Christmas Eve for the rest of her life.

# Chapter Twenty-Four

'Merry Christmas, sweetheart.'

'I'm afraid we're a little short on merry here.' Hal heard Jane sigh over the phone. 'Mum turned the oven on to get the goose cooked but there was a loud cracking sound and black smoke puffed out of the door. Nothing else electrical went bad so I think it's just because the oven is old and we'll need a new one. I'm afraid it'll be sandwiches for lunch.'

'Y'all can come up here to eat.'

'Don't be daft,' she scoffed. 'Poor Sam doesn't need us gate-crashing your Christmas on top of everything else she's got going on.'

'What's wrong?' Mary Ann wandered into the kitchen with little Kerensa tucked into her shoulder.

As soon as he told her the story Hal knew his suggestion would be replaced by his aunt's more forceful steamroller.

She grabbed the phone. 'Get yourselves to Gweal Day now or I'm sendin' Hal to drag you here. We've plenty of room and food comin' out of our ears.' With a triumphant smile she passed the phone back.

'Goodness. She doesn't mince words, does she?' Jane whispered.

'The Muirs are forthright people.' *It's why I told you I love you when we'd only known each other a month*, he thought to himself.

'I'd better break the news to Mum and Nick. Sorry, that came out wrong. I don't mean to sound ungrateful.'

'You're not. Stop beating up on yourself,' Hal tried to

190

reassure her. 'If it was the other way around, wouldn't you invite us all to yours?'

'Well yes but—'

'—but nothing. Argument over. A few more people gathered around the table is the way it should be. I'm sure my aunt is in full-on organising mode by now, so I'd better go help her. Come as soon as you can. Love you.'

'Someone's cheerful. Be warned this will be you one day, son.' Preston ambled into the living room and offered Hal a beer. 'If I've got to wear this in front of other people, I can't be totally sober.'

'Yeah, just lookin' at the thing is bad enough.' He took a swig and wiped his mouth. Mary Ann's present to her husband had to be seen to be believed. The front of the jumper had an impressive set of abs knitted on top of the bright green background with a slogan underneath: "Eat Your Heart out Ross Poldark."

'Ah, there's Gweal Day's answer to Aidan Turner.' Cadan strolled in, laughing.

'A toast to our sweet baby girl.' Preston passed him a bottle too.

'Our daughter will turn into a pickle if you three reprobates drink to her health one more time,' Sam scoffed. Clearly his cousin had moved on from quiet Madonna mode. 'Cadan, we need more of your revolting sprouts from the garden. Preston, you're on extra potato peeling duty.' She jabbed a finger at Hal. 'You can help me lay the table and fetch more chairs.'

'Yes, ma'am.'

'Where's Kerensa?' Cadan frowned.

'Playing with sharp knives in the kitchen of course.'

His wife gave him a pitying look. 'Where on earth do you think she is?'

'Taking a nap?'

'Clever man. Thanks for reminding me why I married you.' Sam breezed out again and ignored Cadan when he shouted after her that no other man would be mad enough to take her on and the next time she wanted Crunchie bars after the local shop was shut not to come running to him.

Would he and Jane be like that? Hal sure hoped so.

'That's the last plate.' Jane dried her hands while the sink emptied. 'I've never seen so many dirty dishes in my life.'

'That's because you haven't been to a full-scale Muir family gathering yet.' Hal dried the plate and added it to the stack. 'I guarantee they'll have one when we go over.' His eyes gleamed and he pulled an envelope from his pocket. 'You get an early present. I didn't want to give you this in front of everyone.'

She pulled out two e-ticket confirmations for a flight from London to Nashville on the third of January.

'Obviously we'll have to travel up from here the day before and I thought we'd stay in Nashville the night we arrive and drive on to Knoxville the next day. That way we won't be complete jet-lagged wrecks.' He looked hesitant. 'Uh did you read all the way through? Like about the return part of the trip.'

Today, wrapped in a happy Christmas bubble, she preferred not to think about how their long-distance relationship would work out. With a heavy heart she did what he asked then gasped. Two return seats booked for the fifteenth.

'Is that okay?'

'Absolutely, more than okay.'

'That's a relief. Day at a time, right?'

Jane wrapped her arms around his neck and kissed him.

'Stop maulin' that girl, Hal Muir.' Mary Ann bustled in. 'She was the one—'

'—don't argue and get those dishes put away. We're gonna open presents before the cute little ole Queen is on the TV at three o'clock. Val told me they never miss it.'

It'd been amusing to see her mother and this feisty lady working together in the kitchen as though they'd known each other for years. Everyone else was given specific tasks and told to stay out of the way when they weren't needed. Suffice to say even after everyone ate until nearly bursting, and beyond in some cases, there were enough leftovers to feed them all for several days. The roasted turkey and goose were the stars but the rest of the meal was an interesting mash-up of both women's traditions. Instead of stuffing they had something similar baked in a dish that Mary Ann called "dressing". Sprouts from Cadan's garden vied with a southern green bean casserole. Roast potatoes went up against candied sweet potatoes. Tiny sausages wrapped in bacon surprised the American visitors, but Mary Ann declared she'd pinch the idea for her next holiday meal. They hadn't even touched the puddings yet.

'We'll be in soon,' Jane promised. 'I assume you know where everything goes, Hal? So you can order me around … for once.'

'Whoa, better make the most of this.'

She flicked his arm with the wet tea towel. 'Behave yourself.'

'Fat chance. That boy's always been trouble.' Mary Ann's smile mitigated the sharp words. 'But if anyone can get him in line it's you, and I reckon he'll be worth it in the long run.'

'Did you treat Cadan this bad?' Hal griped.

'Worse. You're family.'

'Wow, I sure am grateful.' He hugged his aunt. 'I meant that in case you weren't sure.'

'Oh, I got it.'

Jane swallowed back tears as Mary Ann's eyes misted over. Hal hadn't always appreciated his close-knit family but this was his Christmas miracle. 'Don't worry. We both agree that each other is totally worth it, so everything's good,' she reassured his aunt.

'That's all I need to hear.'

'So, do we get high marks when you report back to Hal's parents?' she joked.

'Oh, you'll get ten out of ten, don't worry.' Mary Ann beamed. 'Now come on and hurry up.' A thin wail pierced the air. 'Our little girl is gettin' impatient.'

Hal was having second thoughts. Sam had been reduced to tears when Cadan surprised her with the beautiful desk he'd made and everyone else oohed and aahed over the elegant piece of superb craftsmanship. His own amateurish effort would pale in comparison, but would Jane see past the flaws to the love he'd put into it?

'This one's on the heavy side.' Preston wriggled the awkwardly wrapped present out from under the tree and Hal whipped it out of his uncle's hands.

'It's for you—' he held it out to Jane '—from me.'

'Really?' She pointed at the gift tag and laughed. 'You should be a mystery writer too. I use clues in my books to help readers out. Amazing how well that works.' One quick rip and the paper was gone. 'You made this?'

'Yeah, I've never done any woodwork before … it's not up to Cadan's standards but—' He took the kiss she smacked on his mouth as a good sign '—you said the writing space in your bedroom is always a mess and I thought a desk organiser might help.'

'It's perfect.'

'Cadan designed it.' Hal's face burned. 'He called it minimal which I took to mean easy enough for a novice to put together without too much swearing and aggravation.' One end had a square holder for pens and pencils and the rest consisted of two long, narrow rectangular holders for stationery, Jane's phone and other essentials. 'There were only eight pieces to cut thank goodness.'

'I love this light pine you chose and these details.' She stroked the top edges that he'd picked out in black paint.

'I'll build you a desk to match one day.' His reckless promise made everyone smile. 'Maybe.'

Jane squeezed his hand. 'I'm sure you can do anything you put your mind too.'

The blind faith she had in him stunned Hal.

'Who gets the next present?' Sam jiggled Kerensa who was starting to fuss. 'Someone's gonna want dessert soon.'

'You talking about our daughter or you?' Cadan grinned.

'Hey, I'm a nursing mom I've got to keep my strength up.'

'One Crunchie for her and one for you, right?'

'Something like that.'

They carried on swapping gifts and Hal relaxed on the sofa with his arm around Jane. After he'd opened a soft dark blue jumper from her and a pair of new running shoes, she produced a small wrapped box. 'Pecan Goo-Goo Clusters! Where on earth did you find them?' He ripped one open and sunk his teeth into the marshmallow, nut and chocolate confection, a childhood favourite he'd never grown out of.

Jane grinned. 'We have our methods.' She winked at Mary Ann then lowered her voice to whisper in his ear. 'I'm saving your other gift for later when we're on our own.'

His mind jumped to the red lace underwear.

'That is so not what I meant.' She suppressed a giggle.

'Quiet, everyone.' Mary Ann clapped her hands. 'We're gonna listen to what the Queen has to say then it's time for my pecan pie, boiled custard and snickerdoodle cookies plus Val's Christmas pudding, Christmas cake and mince pies.'

'Lord, I'm gonna need to run a marathon every day between now and when we get on that plane or they'll be loading me as freight,' Hal joked.

'You and me both.'

He risked sneaking a kiss but that set off a round of cheers and encouraging whoops so he gave that up as a bad job.

Jane nervously handed her gift over to Hal. Nine o'clock in the evening on Christmas Day and they were sitting in her living room with only the twinkling Christmas lights on. Finally they were alone. Her mum had been worn out but happy when they returned half an hour ago and went to bed with a cup of tea and the first book in the *Poldark* box set, given to her by Mary Ann of course. Nick had disappeared with a small overnight bag and a sheepish grin when Demelza and her father picked him up to join her family for a late supper. Mr Carter promised to return him to Little Penhaven in time to run with Hal's group in the morning.

'It's not ticking.' He held it to his ear. 'By your petrified expression I wondered if it was goin' to explode.'

'You said ... well, I've never ...'

'All right if I open it or would you like to whisk it away again?'

'Oh, go ahead I suppose.'

Her resignation made him smile and he ripped the paper off, stared at the book and then at her.

'Remember it's only my unedited manuscript and I designed the cover myself just to have something but—'

'Shush.' Hal pressed a finger against her lips. 'This is the most special thing you could give me. You know one day soon you're gonna see your name for real on a proper copy. I predict next year's hot Christmas book will be *Crushed in Cornwall*.' He grinned at the striking cover with a sparkling gold stiletto shoe posed in a pool of blood underneath a Christmas tree. 'Beware of women in high heels?'

'Maybe.'

'It'll be my bedtime reading tonight.'

'If you don't like it, please break it to me gently. I know I've got to develop a tough skin if I'm going to stand a chance at turning this from a hobby into something more but—'

'—that would be like someone telling Cadan and Sam that Kerensa is the ugliest baby they've ever seen?'

'Well, sort of.' It sounded pathetic and she knew it shouldn't matter that much … but it did.

'How about I distract you a little and take your mind off worrying if I'm gonna trash your book?'

As soon as his warm, searching hand hit bare skin under her jumper all Jane could think was *Book? What book?*

# Chapter Twenty-Five

'Your book is bloody unbelievable. You're awesome.'
Hal swept Jane into a hug on her doorstep, hoping she
wouldn't care how hot and sweaty he was after his run.
The teenagers were keeping him on his toes and he and
Tim were amazed at the kids' dedication to keep turning
up every day. 'Damn well kept me up half the night but all
I'm gonna say is if you don't win that competition, they
must be idiots. I'd never have guessed who—'

'—shush. I haven't shown it to anyone else. Remember
this is our secret?' She gave him a firm stare. 'You really
like it? You're not just saying that because we're ... you
know—'

'—in love? Sleepin' together? All of the above?'

'Yes.'

'No. I read a lot of crime novels and—'

'—you never told me that!'

'You didn't ask. Anyway, as I was tryin' to say, I read a lot
and you're now my favourite author.' Hal's insistence made
her smile. 'Look, I'm sorry but I've got to be goin'. This
week's gettin' crazy. Cadan needs my help because they're
trying to bring completion forward on Bluebell Cottage, the
house they're rehabbing. The couple taking it on have been
kicked out of their accommodation and their first baby is
due next month. Poor Cadan only managed to dissuade
Sam from helping by promising I'd step in. My dad isn't a
professional like Preston, but he can turn his hand to about
anythin' and made sure I learned growin' up.'

'I'm at a loose end and I've picked up a few basic skills over the years because we couldn't afford to pay anyone to do jobs around the house, so why don't you let me pitch in too?'

'Sure. That means we see more of each other too, so it's a win all around.'

'Do you want me to throw some old clothes on and come with you now?'

'Sure. No Post-Christmas slump for us. Everyone else is sitting around and stuffing themselves with the leftovers from yesterday.'

'Lazy creatures.' Jane laughed. 'You're lucky I like to be active. Apart from when I'm writing when I'm happy to be glued to my computer for hours, I prefer to be doing something rather than sitting around. I suppose I've never had much free time, so I'm not used to being idle.'

He discovered more about her struggles every day, not that she'd ever call them by that name, but he kept to himself how much he admired her because she was easily embarrassed. 'Yeah, it doesn't suit me either.'

By the evening they were ready to take back their earlier boasts. Mild-mannered Cadan showed his tougher side once they arrived in the nearby village of Nanswarren, bearing his checklist of jobs to be done and detailed instructions from Sam. He set Hal to work ripping out kitchen cabinets while Jane was banished upstairs to repaint the bathroom.

'Are you as exhausted as me?' Hal groaned and stretched out on the sofa. They'd returned back to Jane's house and hadn't had the energy to move again yet. 'I suppose I was using different muscles than normal.' She made a playful grab for his arm and squeezed.

'By New Year's Eve, these should be rippling.'

That was the target date so the house could start the year by welcoming its new occupants and, according to Sam's strict timetable, they should manage it.

'If the bloody rain would stop that'd help,' Jane complained. 'The outdoor painting won't be done at this rate.'

'You're always telling me the Cornish weather is changeable so let's keep our fingers crossed it lives up to its reputation. I hate to leave you now but I need a shower before I meet Tim. I want to run my ideas for starting a programme to engage rural young people in positive activities and focusing on physical fitness by him. It'd start here locally, but I've got big ideas if that's successful. You'd be surprised at some of the conversations we have out running. Gaz isn't a bad kid when you get to know him. His father's rarely there and his mother's a busy lawyer so if he gets in trouble it forces them to pay attention. Of course, it's the wrong sort but in his eyes it's better than being ignored.' Hal reached for her. 'Am I crazy to think I can make a difference?'

'Crazy? No. Over-optimistic? Possibly.' Jane shrugged. 'But if you don't try, you'll never know and if you only help one kid, isn't that worth it?'

'Yeah, you're right.'

'It's like me with my writing. I don't want to regret not giving it a go.'

He tightened his arms around her. 'Encouraging each other. Isn't that what love means when it comes down to it?'

'And you say you're not a "words" sort of man?' Jane's

breathy whisper made him shiver. 'I'll see you tomorrow morning ready for more manual labour but until then ...' The kiss she gave him was brimming with promises, ones he intended to help her keep.

The week had slipped away and the only progress she'd made so far to prepare for their trip was to ask to borrow a suitcase from Heather. Today they'd complete the last finishing touches on Bluebell Cottage, get cleaned up and then head to the pub for the New Year's Eve party.

For probably the twentieth time she re-read the message she'd received this morning.

The Poisoned Chalice finalists will discover their fate as soon as the clock strikes twelve tonight so watch your phones for a text message!

Jane was startled as a horn beeped outside. She hadn't noticed the time slipping away but Hal was always punctual. She dragged on her coat and a woolly hat.

'Don't rush, dear. I think it's for me.' Her mother breezed in from the kitchen.

'I thought you weren't working today?'

'I'm not. I've been invited out for a drive and then I expect we'll have lunch somewhere.'

'We?' Her mum's face turned pink and Jane realised she was wearing the new short grey coat and bright purple silk scarf Jane and Nick bought her for Christmas. 'You're looking nice.'

'Don't sound quite so surprised.'

'Sorry.'

'You're making a mountain out of a ... oh dear that wouldn't be a tactful joke to make.'

She hadn't heard her mum giggle in forever. 'What do you mean?'

'Paul might not like it.'

'Paul who?'

'Paul Burrows of course.'

The penny dropped. 'You're going on a date with Mole Burrows' father?'

'It's not a date.' Val nibbled her lip. 'Well, not really, I mean I'm not sure.' Even after the explanation tripped out Jane wasn't much further ahead. It appeared that Paul Burrows, a retired bus driver who lived near Truro, had come in to the shop one day after visiting his children and got talking to Val. Over the last few weeks he'd come to see Pauline and Terrence more frequently and always found the need to buy something at Jenny's. 'He's a pleasant man who's been widowed a long time and a bit … lonely, like me.'

Why had she assumed that because Ralph Davy turned out to be no good that her mother considered herself well rid of men?

'That's lovely. I've only met him a few times, but he seems a nice man.'

'Thank you.'

'What for?'

'Not saying I'm being old and silly.'

'Good grief, Mum. You're only sixty and if anyone deserves a bit of happiness it's you. Everyone does.' Jane pushed her towards the door. 'Have a wonderful time. Will you both be at the pub tonight?'

'Of course. Apart from anything else, you said you'd find out the writing competition result later and I'm not going to miss that.'

Jane's stomach plummeted. The prospect of being humiliated in front of her family and friends hadn't occurred to her. She'd prefer to deal with her disappointment in private and break the news her own way afterwards.

'Oh, lovey.' Her mum must have noticed the change in her expression. 'We're all rooting for you to win but we're so proud you've made it this far.'

*Exactly what Hal would say*, she thought. 'I know.'

'I'd better go, or Paul will think I've stood him up.' Val hugged her. 'We'll see you later. Nick said he and Demelza are working at the pub tonight.'

'Have a great time.'

It was hard to believe that this time last month she felt guilty for starting a relationship with Hal when she felt she should be focusing on helping out her mother and brother. She wasn't the only one whose life had changed.

'What, no paint under your fingernails?' Hal scrutinised Jane's hands. 'I was getting used to it.'

In theory the whole of Little Penhaven couldn't really be here, but it sure felt like it. Sam and Cadan hadn't wanted to bring Kerensa to the crowded pub and said they were too exhausted to stay awake until midnight anyway. They'd packed Mary Ann and Preston off with Hal to experience the traditional village way of wrapping up another year. Some people would go to the short church service first, whereas others would wait out the early evening at home but everyone who was physically able to make it would gather in Fore Street before midnight and count down the last few seconds of the year together. The village had no money for official fireworks, but a few locals would set off their own as the church bells struck the hour.

'That colour blue didn't match my jumper.'

'Picky woman.'

She slid her arms around his waist. 'Yes, I'm picky. Do you have a problem with that?'

'Nah, as long as you keep on pickin' me.'

'I don't usually make New Year resolutions but that's one I'm happy to make.'

Hal kissed her and, for once, they didn't get mocked because everyone else was too busy getting into the party spirit.

'I don't know how Fliss and Jory are still standing. They've hardly had a moment to draw breath for the last month or so.' Jane shook her head.

'Cadan told me that John Pickering is stepping back in to run the place for a couple of weeks so they can have a holiday. They're off to Hawaii tomorrow. I think it's a Christmas present from her folks.'

'I'm sure Jory can't wait to get back on his surfboard.' She gave Hal a quizzical look. 'Do you surf?'

'Not very well. I know it's a Californian thing, but I didn't grow up around beaches and I'm more comfortable in the mountains. You?' Hal could've kicked himself. As if she'd ever had the money or time to indulge in that sort of luxury. 'Sorry I—'

'—don't apologise. You're right, I've never had the chance.'

'Maybe we can give it a try together next summer?'

'I'd like that.' She blushed. 'But that's true of pretty much anything we do together.'

'Snap.'

The pub was thinning out, and Jane frowned when he glanced at his watch. 'Come on, let's head on outside with everyone else. Don't fret. You'll see your phone screen light up when the message arrives.' Hal gripped her hand and steered her out before she could protest.

Preston waved from across the street where they'd staked a spot outside the Chinese restaurant. Nick was already there with Demelza, Val and Paul Burrows. When they'd met earlier, Paul had struck him as a decent man. Jane was still slightly bemused by the turn of events but happy to see her mother's obvious pleasure in Paul's company.

When the church clock struck once everyone started to count down. As the twelfth chime rang out, they all cheered and yelled and the street was a mass of people kissing and hugging. Hal swept Jane into his arms and kissed her.

'Happy New Year.'

'Happy New Year, Hal.' Her kiss left him in no doubt it would be, but Jane suddenly turned pale and stared at her phone. 'Oh God, I can't look.'

'Do you want me to?'

'Yes … No … I don't know.'

'Is everything okay?' Val was now beside them, obviously realising the important text had arrived.

Jane pointed to her phone.

'It won't read itself, lovey.'

The determination that got her this far in the first place seemed to return. She let go of him and scrolled through the message. First her face fell but a few seconds later a brilliant smile lit her up.

'Good news. Bad news,' she quipped. 'I didn't win but I'm the runner up and the judges loved my manuscript so much they've offered me a publication deal too.'

'I knew you'd do it.' Hal swept her off her feet, swung her around and kissed her hard.

Word spread as it always did in Little Penhaven and soon people were gathered around congratulating Jane. It took a while for things to calm down before some went back into the pub and others headed for home.

'We're staying to clear up,' Nick said. 'Demelza's dad's picking us up later, and I'm going back to hers and staying for a party they're having tomorrow lunchtime.'

*Yes.*

'Paul's giving me a lift home. We'll see you … whenever.' Val's eyes gleamed.

*Even better.*

Mary Ann gave a broad smile. 'Cynthia and George have invited us to join them and a few of their friends for champagne at their house. She's offered us their spare room for the night, so you don't have to worry about runnin' us home later.'

He didn't deserve this much luck, but he'd grab it with both hands. 'How about you joinin' me at Gweal Day?' In the dark he sensed Jane blush. 'I'm sure Sam and Cadan crashed out hours ago.'

'You've talked me into it … again. Seems to be a habit of yours.'

'Was that a complaint?'

'Hardly.' She laughed and took his hand. 'Come on. We're wasting time.'

\*

With the New Year less than an hour old she sat on a bench outside Gweal Day being kept warm by Hal's arms around her, unable to imagine how much better life could get than this but pretty sure this was only the start of something incredibly wonderful. How could she have been so wrong? The dismissive way she'd described Hal when Sam first showed the SAPs his picture filled her head; a huge man with gleaming white teeth, thick dark blond hair, bright blue eyes and muscular arms folded over a massive chest positively oozing cockiness.

Talk about not judging a book by its cover.

'Time to enjoy our own celebration.' Hal popped the cork on the bottle of champagne he'd brought out from the farmhouse and poured them both a drink. 'Here's to us and the future.'

'Are you glad you followed Sam's example?'

'No, bloody miserable. Can't you tell? For a genius writer, you're not very observant.'

Jane drained her glass. 'I suggest we move the party inside. It's getting cold and although you're an amazing hugger, I think we could … enjoy ourselves more in the warm.'

'There's always—'

'—no, I'm not into woodwork sheds. That's Sam's thing not mine. I'd rather celebrate the beginning of our New Year surrounded by twinkling fairy lights and you.'

'Yes, ma'am. Happy to oblige.' Hal knocked back his drink, set down the glass and scooped her up into his arms.

# Thank You

I'm thankful for all of you wonderful people who've read this story and I hope that visiting Little Penhaven at Christmas was a welcome break away from everyday life. If you've enjoyed Jane and Hal's story and have a minute to leave a review at the retail site where you purchased your book that would be wonderful.

Angela

x

# About the Author

Angela was born in St. Stephen, Cornwall, England. After completing her A-Levels she worked as a Naval Secretary. She met her husband, a US Naval Flight Officer while being based at a small NATO Headquarters on the Jutland Peninsula in Denmark. They lived together in Denmark, Sicily, California, southern Maryland and London before settling in Franklin, Tennessee.

Angela took a creative writing course in 2000 and loved it so much that she has barely put her pen down since. She has had short stories and novels published in the US. Her debut novel, *Sugar & Spice*, won Choc Lit's Search for an American Star competition and is her UK debut.

### Follow Angela:

Blog: www.angelabritnellromance.com
Twitter: www.twitter.com/AngelaBritnell
Facebook: www.facebook.com/angelabritnell

# More Choc Lit

*From Angela Britnell*

## One Summer in Little Penhaven

**Could one summer change your life?**
When high-flying American lawyer Samantha Muir finds out she's lost her partnership whilst on an assignment in London, she has a dramatic reaction. Rather than returning home, she resigns, leaves her business suits behind and jumps on the first train to Cornwall at the encouragement of a friendly stranger.

The village of Little Penhaven, where Samantha eventually ends up, is a world away from her life in Knoxville, Tennessee - and local farmer Cadan Day is certainly a world away from any man she has met before. But could the Cornish village and Cadan play a part in Samantha's summer of self-discovery?

*Prequel to Christmas in Little Penhaven*

## Christmas at Black Cherry Retreat

**What if you had nowhere to call home for Christmas?**
When Fee Winter books a winter break at the remote Black Cherry Retreat in the small town of Pine Ridge, Tennessee, it's with the idea that the peace and quiet will help her recuperate from her hectic life as a photographer.

But what she didn't bank on was meeting Tom Chambers and his huge, interfering yet lovable family. With them, could Fee finally experience the warmth and support that's been missing from her own life – and maybe even find a place to call home in time for Christmas?

## Sugar and Spice

### The Way to a Hero's Heart …

Fiery, workaholic Lily Redman wants more than anything to make a success of her new American TV show, Celebrity Chef Swap – without the help of her cheating ex-fiancé and producer, Patrick O'Brien. So when she arrives in Cornwall, she's determined to do just that.

Kenan Rowse is definitely not looking for love. Back from a military stint in Afghanistan and recovering from a messy divorce, the last thing he needs is another complication. So when he lands a temporary job as Luscious Lily's driver, he's none too pleased to find that they can't keep their hands off each other!

But trudging around Cornish farms, knee deep in mud, and meetings with egotistical chefs was never going to be the perfect recipe for love – was it? And Lily could never fall for a man so disinterested in food – could she?

## What Happens in Nashville

### 'What happens in Nashville, stays in Nashville!'

Claire Buchan is hardly over the moon about the prospect of her sister's hen party; travelling from the UK to Nashville, Tennessee, for a week of honky-tonks, karaoke and cowboys. Certainly not straight-laced Claire's idea of a good time, what with her lawyer job and sensible boyfriend, Philip.

But then she doesn't bank on meeting Rafe Castello. As he and Claire get to know each other, she realises there is far more to him than meets the eye.

Can Claire keep to the holiday mantra of 'what happens in Nashville, stays in Nashville' or will she find that some things are far too difficult to simply leave behind?

## Celtic Love Knot

**Can two tangled lives make a love knot?**
Lanyon Tremayne is the outcast of his small Cornish village of St. Agnes. Nobody knows the painful secret he hides.

Olivia Harding has learnt a thing or two about ogres. She's a professor from Tennessee, specialising in Celtic mythology and has come to St. Agnes to research the legend of a Cornish giant – and to lay to rest a couple of painful secrets of her own.

But when Olivia meets the ruggedly handsome Lanyon, her trip to Cornwall looks set to become even more interesting. Will she get through to the man beneath the bad-tempered façade, or is Lanyon fated to be the 'ogre' of St. Agnes forever?

## The Wedding Reject Table

**Once on the reject table, always on the reject table?**
When Maggie Taylor, a cake decorator, and Chad Robertson, a lawyer from Nashville Tennessee, meet at a wedding in Cornwall it's not under the best circumstances.

They have both been assigned to 'the reject table', alongside a toxic collection of grumpy great aunts, bitter divorcees and stuffy organists.

Maggie has grown used to being the reject, although when Chad helps her out of a wedding cake disaster she begins to wonder whether the future could hold more for her.

But will Chad be strong enough to deal with the other problems in Maggie's life? Because a ruined cake isn't the only issue she has – not by a long shot.

## Here Comes the Best Man

**Being the best man is a lot to live up to …**
When troubled army veteran and musician
Josh Robertson returns home to Nashville
to be the best man at his younger brother
Chad's wedding he's just sure that he's going
to mess it all up somehow.

But when it becomes clear that the
wedding might not be going to plan, it's
up to Josh and fellow guest Louise Giles
to make sure that Chad and his wife-to-be
Maggie get their perfect day.

Can Josh be the best man his brother
needs? And is there somebody else who is
beginning to realise that Josh could be her
'best man' too?

## Love Me for a Reason

**Love doesn't always have to make sense …**
When Daisy Penvean meets Nathaniel
Dalton whilst visiting a friend in Nashville, it
seems there are a million and one reasons for
them not to be together. Nathaniel's job as
a mergers and acquisitions manager means
sharp suits and immaculate hair, whereas
Daisy's work as a children's book illustrator
lends itself to a more carefree, laid-back
style. And, as Daisy lives in England, there's
also the small matter of the Atlantic Ocean
between them.

But when Nathaniel's job takes him to
London, he and Daisy meet again under very
different circumstances. Because Daisy works
for the publisher involved in the deal, and
if Nathaniel does his job, it could mean she
loses hers …

## You're The One That I Want

**What if you didn't want to fake it any more?**
When Sarah, a teacher from Cornwall, and Matt, a businessman from Nashville, meet on a European coach tour, they soon find themselves in a relationship …

Except it's a fake relationship. Because Matt is too busy for romance, and Sarah is only trying to make her cheating ex-husband jealous … isn't she?

As Matt and Sarah complete their tour of Europe, they do all the things real couples are supposed to do.

But as their holiday comes to an end, Sarah and Matt realise that they're not happy with their pretend relationship. They want the real thing.

## New Year New Guy

**Out with the old life, in with the new …**
When Laura's bride-to-be sister, Polly, organises a surprise reunion for her fiancé and his long lost American friend, Laura grudgingly agrees to help keep the secret. And when the plain-spoken, larger-than-life Hunter McQueen steps off the bus in her rainy Devon town and only just squeezes into her tiny car, it confirms that Laura has made a big mistake in going along with her sister's crazy plan.

But could the tall, handsome man with the Nashville drawl be just what reserved Laura Williams needs to shake up her life and start something new?

## A Summer to Remember in Herring Bay

Essy Havers is good at finding things. Her company specialises in helping clients track down anything, from missing china pieces to rare vintage clothing. But now Essy has something more important to find: herself.

Essy has always been curious about her mother's secret past and her Cornish roots. So, when the opportunity arises, she hops on a plane in Tennessee and ends up in Herring Bay in Cornwall; the village where her mother grew up.

But once there, she's mystified by the reactions of the villagers when they realise who she is. Was Essy's decision to visit Cornwall a mistake, or will it lead to a summer she'll never forget?

## Christmas at Moonshine Hollow

**Mistletoe and moonshine: a Christmas match made in heaven?**
Moonshine Hollow's famous 'Lightning Flash' might be an acquired taste, although the same could be said for moonshine distillery owner Cole Landon, what with his workaholic habits and 'Scrooge' tendencies when it comes to all things Christmassy.

But when Jenna Pendean from Cornwall pays a visit to Cole's family-run distillery in Tennessee during the holiday season, will Cole's cynicism about the existence of Christmas miracles be put to the test?

## A Cornish Summer at Pear Tree Farm

**Cornish charm and a Tennessee twist – the perfect pair?**

Nessa Vivian is determined to keep her parents' business afloat, but Pear Tree Farm near the backwater Cornish village of Polgarth didn't do well as farm, and it's not faring much better as a camp site. Maybe it's due to Nessa's habit of taking in troubled runaways, like ex-soldier Crispin, for next to nothing. Or perhaps her highly-strung sister Lowena is right – caravans named after Beatles' songs and homegrown pears are not enough to turn the farm into a tourist haven.

Then another troubled runaway turns up, posing the greatest threat yet. Ex-musician Ward Spencer from Tennessee is certainly intriguing, but could his plans to put nearby Tregereth House on the map mean Pear Tree Farm is finished – or does his arrival signal a second lease of life, and not just for Nessa's business?

## Spring on Rendezvous Lane

**Can even the most seasoned traveller find a home on Rendezvous Lane?**

'Community spirit' is not a phrase in travel junkie Taran Rossi's vocabulary. As a former 'third culture kid' and now spicy street food connoisseur and social media influencer, he's never really stayed in one place long enough to feel part of a community. And that's just the way he likes it. But a springtime stint house sitting for his grandmother on Rendezvous Lane in East Nashville could lead to a long overdue wake-up call. With the help of single mum Sandy Warner and her young son Chip, can Taran come to understand that sometimes it's not about the place – it's about the people?

# Introducing Choc Lit